a breath too late

a
breath
too
late

ROCKY CALLEN

HENRY HOLT AND COMPANY
NEW YORK

Henry Holt and Company
Publishers since 1866
Henry Holt® is a registered trademark of Macmillan Publishing Group, LLC
120 Broadway, New York, NY 10271 • fiercereads.com

Library of Congress Control Number: 2019949141
ISBN 978-1-250-23879-5

Our books may be purchased in bulk for promotional, educational, or
business use. Please contact your local bookseller or the Macmillan Corporate
and Premium Sales Department at (800) 221-7945 ext. 5442 or by email at
MacmillanSpecialMarkets@macmillan.com.

First edition, 2020 / Designed by Katie Klimowicz
Printed in the United States of America
1   3   5   7   9   10   8   6   4   2

For the ones wandering in the dark.
Don't forget that the stars are yours too.

Disclaimer: This novel contains descriptions of physical abuse and deals with the topics of suicide and depression.

Author's Note

Suicide happens every day. Every minute. It is estimated that worldwide nearly a million people lose their lives each year.

One million fathers, mothers, sisters, brothers, sons, daughters who are lost because they felt they had no hope left.

This novel isn't about happy endings. It is about the beautiful and terrible moments that make up a life and the possibilities that live in even the darkest of places that sometimes we are just too blind to see.

I am asking you to look closer, look deeper, look everywhere, and be audacious and tenacious in your quest to find that hope in your life. Because you are wondrous and the world needs you in it.

I worked as a behavioral therapist for more than a decade and I have grappled with high-functioning depression since I was a child. I also have known cycles of abuse left secret. The variance of our experience, the nuances of our pain, the complexities of these issues are endless.

The moment the truth is out, you can't shove it back

into its shadowy corner. And the truth is, there are days when I feel unstoppable, days when my pockets are lined with sunshine and possibilities, and then there are days when I feel there are anchors tied to my ankles and I am sinking and no one can see me drowning.

I wrote this book because I needed it. I almost made the same choice Ellie made when I was eleven years old. But every time I got lost in the labyrinth of my own heartache or suffering, I would stumble out to find a life waiting for me, a life that was mine, a life I wanted to keep.

And as a behavioral therapist, I saw the extraordinary strength and tenacity of the human spirit.

In my work and in my life, I have come to realize:

Hope can be found in the darkness.

Depression can sometimes surge and hold me hostage, but it is my vehement belief that tomorrow will matter, and so I remain vigilant in caring for my mental and emotional health in order to break free.

I wrote this book for the people who have kept their pain secret, for those who have shuttered their hearts and their doors, for those who might not see the hope that is reaching for them.

This book cannot be everything I want it to be, but it can be this: a reminder that you don't have to be alone, that help exists and is waiting, and that the only way we can change the statistic of suicide and domestic violence is if we break the silence with our stories.

This book is for the Ellies of the world who we have lost,

the ones left behind whose hearts are mending, and those teetering on the edge between hope and pain.

And if that is you, I see you.

Please stay.

Again, I say this to you (because I have often had to remember it myself): The world needs you in it.

1

Death,

As blackness eats my last sliver of consciousness, I realize I regret.

You aren't beautiful, free, or romantic like in all of the novels I have read. You are a girl who had no hope left, who realized, too late, she wanted to live. I thought you would save me, Death.

But you are a liar.

Just like everyone else.

2

Life,

You are too quiet. The kind of quiet that isn't quiet at all. It is the smothering silence that bleeds into everything; the kind of absence that mocks, prods, and stares you down until you are withered to your bones.

I had the worst dream last night, but I can't quite remember it. I feel groggy. The dream settles into something dim and far away and yet it scratches at me, it curls a finger in my direction and beckons me closer. I ignore it.

The room still looks dark, too dark. My alarm went off, didn't it?

I rub my eyes and pad my way toward the door. I like

to be downstairs before Momma and Father. I blink when I flip the switch in the hallway. Dark. Still dark? Maybe the lights burned out or maybe Momma didn't pay the electricity bill again. I swear under my breath. I step lightly, leaning my weight on the railing so I don't make the stairs creak too much. I rub my eyes again. The sleep still must be in them, because nothing looks quite right.

I bump the Alaska snow globe on the side of the vanity next to the base of the stairs and I frantically reach out to catch it, but it sits still in its spot. I blink, confused, and then exhale loudly as I turn the corner and freeze.

Momma and Father are already in the kitchen, sitting in the dark.

I rub my arm with my palm and step inside the kitchen. They don't look up. They never do. I take the long way around to the cabinets, not going straight from the door to the counters because that would brush me up against Father's chair. I walk around, squeezing instead behind Momma. Regina. Her name means queen, but you would never know it. She's a tall thing in a small space, crammed in where she doesn't quite fit.

I flinch seeing her. Something is wrong, very wrong. She is practically a corpse, quiet, still, black and blue painting her face as if she's already rotting. She's not wearing makeup. She never comes downstairs without makeup on to cover up the bruises. Never.

I wish I could hate her, but I can't.

I brush past her and open the cabinets before sitting. I want to ask why they are sitting in the dark, but I don't want to be the one to break the silence, shatter it into tiny pieces, because at least the silence can't hurt you. I keep my mouth shut.

No wonder I like hard-core metal. The band members can scream until their throats are hoarse, while my throat is dry and aching from hardly ever making a sound. Father is sitting at the table, waiting. Watching. Momma's eyes are cast down.

She whimpers.

I tense. She never, ever makes a sound . . . not even when I hear the slaps and the pounding through the bedroom walls, not even when the punches slam into her. Never a whimper, never a sound.

I look at her, really look at her. Her eyes are bloodshot. Her skin is red and blotchy, along with the normal blacks and blues and fading yellows. Her eyes are practically swollen shut. I want to reach my hand to hers, but I don't.

Whatever thing is breaking her, I won't break too. The thought bites at me even as I feel ashamed. I still watch her from under my eyelashes and see she is clutching something in her hands. I stare at it. It is no larger than the height of her hand. A stuffed teddy bear with an eye hanging on by a thread wearing a tiny T-shirt that says SOMEONE IN BALTIMORE LOVES ME.

She's been in my room. The bear was on my bed, beside the pillow. I want to reach over and snatch it from her. I

4

almost do, but then she whimpers again, a throaty, gurgling sound following it. She is holding her breath to keep the sob down. She isn't trying hard enough.

Father looks at her. Rolls back his shoulders in that slow, deliberate way of his and then leans forward across the table. "Oh, Regina." His voice is smooth, deceitfully soothing. "Stop that crying. It isn't your fault." Father stands up and Momma flinches just as she hiccups the tears down. He's dragging his chair behind him until he pushes it next to Momma. The scratches against the floor grate against my ears. He sits down slowly and says, "Shhhhh, you know I don't like to hear you cry."

A warning. A warning cloaked in comfort. He is about to strike. I can feel it. I start to shift away in my chair. About to run. He doesn't like to hear her cry and when she does, he gives her a reason to cry harder.

She ignores the warning.

The sobs come, fierce and splintering like an earthquake. My eyes widen as I jerk my gaze to her. I stand up and lunge for the doorway. I have to get away, to escape the pull of the crevasse she is creating with her tears. She is going to drag me down. I can feel it. It isn't normal, the way she cries. It scares me.

Momma clutches the bear to her chest. She knows what's coming, but she doesn't stop crying. Father growls and pushes her against the wall, her chair tipping back underneath her, and then puts one massive hand over her throat. His own body is crushing her against the wall. He's always crushing something. Momma wheezes out her stuttering sobs and she's shaking.

"Shhhhh, shhhhhh. It's okay. I got you. You just have to listen to me. Okay? Shhh."

Mom's jerkily shaking her head side to side. She's saying no. She's saying stop. She's saying help.

But I don't.

I run. I run outside. Momma must have pushed or resisted because now I hear her wails again. Father is shouting. Glass is shattering. There is a tornado behind me and I don't stop running. I gulp in the air, heaving frantically. I must've been holding my breath.

There are no bruises, or secrets, or screams out here on the sidewalk. I sigh and pull out my headphones. I turn up the volume all the way, ignoring the warning about hearing loss that pops up on the screen. I keep my finger on the volume button even though it says MAX, just in case I can squeeze out a bit more noise. *C'mon*, I think. *Just a little louder. Just make the world go away.*

My shoulders relax as the electric guitars roar, the drums thud ferociously, and the lead singer screams into the mic.

It doesn't get louder. The world doesn't go away and within ten minutes, I face my school.

I rub my arms. It is cold for May. It's overcast. The sky somehow seems bright, but filtered, like an Instagram photo where they offset the image so it has softer, muted colors. I

6

cock my head to the side and try to blink it away, but as I make my way up the school steps, I glance to the right.

He is there.

I don't pause or even let my eyes linger. I just catch him looking up and staring, searching the sidewalk. I grit my teeth for a minute as I charge up the stairs.

Of course, he is searching for someone. Someone else. Someone without bruises under her T-shirt or death-metal music companions to drown out the world. He is of this world—wholly. Some strange mix of geek and rocker, intelligent and artistic, cool, but not so cool as to be an ass about it. August Matthews.

I kind of like the fact that his name is a month of the year, a month of sunlight, humid air, lightning bugs, last parties, beach trips, and my birthday.

I chance one last glance at him as I open the door. He is still there, expectant, waiting. Just not for me.

I walk inside and don't look back. It seems like yesterday that it was me he was waiting for on the sidewalk.

That strange, uncollected feeling hits me again.

A loss of time, of a sequence of events. *Was it really yesterday?* I feel like I am midstep and losing my balance, unsteady. I try to remember clearly, but the memory feels hazy. *No, of course not. That was years ago.* But even as I accept that teetering thought, it feels uncertain.

Students are already filing into their first period. The first alarm blares. I frown. How am I late?

I make my way to English Lit, the only bearable class in high school—partly because I want to be a writer when I leave this hellhole and partly because I like the teacher, Ms. Hooper. When she recites a passage from a book, her eyes sparkle as if somehow the words make her more real, like they're her talisman and she just needs to read them to be set on fire. I wonder if she can feel it. The twinkle of life, I mean. I wonder if it's something that bubbles up inside her. I wonder what that must feel like.

I want to be Ms. Hooper.

Eyeing August's empty place just a couple of seats away, I sit down. Sometimes I think I feel him watching me, but that's stupid. He wouldn't watch me. Not like before, especially with Ms. Hooper twinkling with so much life and me rotting in my chair.

I sit down, surprised Britney doesn't make her oh-my-gosh-I-can't-believe-I-am-sitting-next-to-this-freak eyes at me. She just giggles with Sarah and Terry and then they squeeze into their respective seats, ignoring me entirely. Which is fine by me. I am perfectly happy being ignored.

I stretch and look up at the ceiling. There are thirty-six cracks up there. I know. I've counted them all.

The door creaks open and I shift my gaze to the doorway. August is there, breathless. He looks confused and flustered, which doesn't suit him. He makes his way to his seat and then knocks his knuckles on my desk while chancing a glance at the door again.

I blink at the spot where his knuckles had been. What was that about?

I stiffen in my chair and look back. August's eyes are on the door as he twirls a pencil with his fingers. He always has one in his hand or tucked behind his ear. Always ready to draw something in his sketch pad. He needs to be ready for when the muse hits. I used to tease him about it when we were younger.

I pivot forward, feeling woozy all of a sudden. Ms. Hooper is leaning against her desk, hands clasped in front of her. She is young and beautiful, but she isn't glittering with her usual splendor. Her jaw is too tight, her eyes not sparkly at all. I can see how she swallows over and over again as if she has something to say and is struggling to get the words out.

Does anyone else notice? I glance around. There is not a single face looking up at Ms. Hooper. They are ducked down staring at phone screens or leaning across desks to mouth something to their friends. August is tapping his leg against his desk, still watching the door. Who is he waiting for?

Ms. Hooper finally clears her throat, just barely grabbing the students' attention. She looks at me. I perk up. *Yes, I'm listening. I am here.*

Beautiful and twinkling people have this way about them. A way that makes you feel like if they just watched you, just connected, you would somehow be a bit more twinkly too. She doesn't twinkle at me though, so I can't twinkle back. She stares through me, eyes glassy, and I am convinced that somehow the black void of emptiness inside me must've robbed her of that beautiful dazzle and sent it off into the ether where so many things are lost, including, but not exclusively, my smile.

Ms. Hooper finally speaks. "Class, quiet." There is an edge to her voice I have never heard before. I stiffen, wondering who might've cheated on our last test on Friday. I scan the room. Becca or Ty? I stare at the couple in the front corner. Eyes red, goofy grins, and gazes far-off and distant. Stoned? Really? At 7:45 a.m.? I roll my eyes. I am surrounded by idiots.

Ms. Hooper clears her throat again. "I—I have a very sad announcement today. One of your classmates"—her voice breaks—"died yesterday."

Her face turns red and splotchy and I sit up straighter. Died? Someone died? I scroll through my own mental roster of students and try to remember who I saw in the hallways.

The classroom is silent.

Ms. Hooper continues, "Ellie Walker"—her voice cracks again—"died by suicide in her home yesterday."

There is silence. Too much of it.

My heart is knocking against my rib cage, breaking it.

No.

No-no-no-no-no. I am standing and about to scream, *I am right here!*

Ready to throw this desk at someone. Anyone. To get their attention. To make them see.

But someone is already shouting. I whip my head to the side. August is standing and yelling, pointing one accusatory finger at Ms. Hooper. "You are lying! You are fucking lying!"

I have never heard August swear.

Or yell.

Or heard his voice made of splinters and ragged edges.

That's when I feel it. The absolute offness of it all. The otherness of everything around me and how I don't quite fit in this world.

Ms. Hooper's arms are raised as if she is coaxing a scared animal to calm down and as she does, August covers his face with his hands.

He's shaking. So am I.

And I can't stay in here. I can't hold my breath any longer. I need to breathe. So I run.

I go to the girls' bathroom, lungs aching from exertion. I stare into the mirror . . .

And see nothing.

I scream.

And no one can hear me.

3

Memory,

I am trying to hold you, but you keep slipping through my fingertips.

4

Momma,

I run home, lungs heaving with each breath, and stag-
ger up to my room. I don't open my eyes at first. They are
clenched shut, afraid.

Breathe in. Breathe out.

I open my eyes.

I remember . . .

The way my breathing was short and shallow as I tied
the knot. I was moving fast. I was nervous. My fingers kept
fumbling. My fingers didn't want to die. They knew better
than my brain, better than my breaking heart. I lean against
the doorframe.

My gaze falls to my feet. They are bare. I blink. Hadn't I been dressed? I seek out my inked-up Converse shoes, the shoes that were supposed to take me places, and as I reach for them, my hands pass right through them.

I. Am. Dead.

I collapse onto the floor. Our row house is long and narrow, as if it is squished on its sides. I feel it pressing in. The walls are going to suffocate me.

Beside the chair is a metal bowl with charred ashes. I blink. I don't remember that bowl. Don't remember what could have burned inside it. I crawl over to look. I reach in to try to pluck some of the uncharred bits of paper out of it and my hand drifts through it. I fall back on my feet and let out a shuddering breath.

The world and I are no longer of each other. It isn't mine anymore.

I grit my teeth. *It was never mine.*

My head falls into my hands and I rub my temples, fighting to remember. I had thoughts of suicide all the time. Passing thoughts. They had felt tender and secret, but I don't remember that moment—that moment when it wasn't just a thought but a secret monster made real.

My mind is a jumble of images and memories and I can't put them together in the right order. Time feels disjointed and I can't hold it.

It is only then, me on the floor and looking over to my bed, that I see how the mattress caves in the middle. There is a heavy weight on it. I push up to my knees and see someone curled up, facing the wall.

I blink.

Standing up, I see that it is you, Momma.

You look too big for my mattress. You were so much taller than me. Your knees are tucked up by your chin and you're asleep. I circle the bed so I can see you more clearly. Your lower lip is split and starting to scab over. I can see the blood crusted on the inside of your nostril.

Your head is on my pillow. I want you out. I want you away! I want to be on my own bed with my room locked.

But then I see you are still holding my bear.

And it is such a sweet and tender feeling that swells in my chest unbidden.

You had bought me that bear when we moved here. Just me and you and this house on Sunset Street. His fur had been a rich golden-brown and he had two sparkling black eyes. You got it when we drove through Baltimore. It was *the fluffiest, fuzziest, and cuddliest one* you had said, *for my cuddliest little girl.* I remember squealing in delight when you gave it to me. I sat in my booster seat and I used my bear as a pillow as we made the long drive to our new home with the car windows open—air and sunlight pouring in.

I inhale as the sunlight sputters out of the memory.

The bear has matted fur now. It is tearing at the seams. It looks old and raggedy. I needed to squeeze it tight for too long for comfort. And now there is hardly anything left to hold.

I step away from the bed and clench my fists. I don't want to forgive you. You kept us here. You let him in. I don't care how much you cry. You are too late.

You are years too late. But then, you are the one breathing and I am the one who isn't. An itch comes to my mind: *You were too afraid to leave. I was too afraid to stay.*

The thought is a bullet to my chest, splitting me open, and a fresh rage roars inside me. I punch the wall, but my hand just flies through it and I swear. I didn't swear often when I was alive, but in this moment when I am just a smudge among other gray shadows, I use up the entire dictionary of expletives.

I want to break this world into pieces and I can't even make a dent.

The world isn't mine, I think again.

It never was.

5

Momma,

After my monologue of swear words, I am exhausted. It doesn't stop me from trying to reach back into the real world, though. I try grabbing you, to shake you, but nothing I do lets me reconnect. I yell in frustration until finally I just collapse against the wall, sliding to the ground to curl up on the floor.

I am an idiot. An idiot! I should've just left. Run away. Ditched this house that smelled of whiskey and cigarettes and too much sweat. Abandoned this house of controlling gazes, fierce punches, and too much quiet.

I recognize the cold sweat that trickles between my

shoulder blades and the way my breath hiccups even though I don't need any breath in my lungs. I wonder if those church ladies were right. A suicide case goes to hell. On top of that, I am a bastard child and I will be set squarely in the unconsecrated ground come my funeral.

My funeral? Isn't that what you should be doing, Momma? Or did it already happen?

I stare at the bed. You are still curled up like a baby.

Is that why I am still here? In this in-between, in this smudgy, unreal place? Have I not been put to rest yet? Is it because I wasn't baptized? Is this all a dream?

My head aches. I walk into the bathroom and stare in the mirror. At first, I don't see anything, but then slowly, probably because I know I am there, the edges of me solidify and my features become clearer. My skin tone is ashen. My eyes just a shade too pale and my bone structure looks more pronounced. Is this what being dead looks like? I lean in closer and stare.

I stare as if my reflection will hand me answers, tell me why, tell me what to do now. But it doesn't. "Tell me!" I scream.

The doorbell ring startles me. My head jerks toward the bathroom door and the shrill sound. A doorbell? I didn't even know the doorbell still worked. No one comes to our house tucked between the two vacant row houses on Sunset Street.

I creep out into the hallway as if someone could actually

18

spot me. They can't, obviously. I am a ghost. At least I think I am. Nevertheless, I still creep. Quiet. Hesitant. I walk down the stairs to look out the window to see who is on our front porch. I inhale at seeing the familiar hunch of his shoulders and the way his hair falls into his eyes.

August. His hands are shoved in his pockets and he waits, clenching his jaw. He swallows hard and knocks. He looks at the driveway, sees the mismatched colored doors of your minivan barely holding on to its own life, and then bangs on the door harder. He knows someone is here.

I am here. August is on my front porch and I am here, forcing my hand to stay put against the glass so it doesn't slide through. I want this to be real. My eyes beg to be seen.

He looks toward the window and I gasp as his gaze travels over the very spot where I stand. But then it slides right past me. He bangs again. I hear you moan upstairs and the mattress creaks. I bristle, thinking about how the movements in my room echo throughout the house. I never knew that. It was good that I cried into my pillow.

It was good that I learned to be quiet and hold my breath, because the house could hear all of our secrets.

You are stumbling down the stairs. You squint, trying to make August's face out through the cloth-covered glass until finally you call, "Who is it?" Your voice is too weak the first time. It rasps out. So you call again, this time after clearing your throat. "Who is it?"

"Hello, Ms. Walker? I, I am August Ma—"

You crack open the door and look through it with your one non-bruised eye. "I know who you are." It sounds like an accusation when you say it, but I don't know why.

"I . . . I . . . just heard . . ." He trails off. I stare at him. He looks so much younger than what I remember. Did he just want to see if this was a prank? Real? What was he expecting? I try to remember the last time he was on our porch and can't. I try to remember the last time we spoke, but where there should be memories to turn to, there is only fog. Something's there, itching at my mind, but nothing reaches out to illuminate me.

He waits for you to speak. I can see it on his face. But you don't say a word.

He finally says it. "Is . . . is it true? About Ellie?"

You stare at him dazed, as if you are confused. As if you can't quite piece together the English language anymore. With the subtlest of motions, you nod and close the door, locking the boy and his realness out, and keeping us tucked in here where it looks like you're trying to pretend that I am just somewhere in the house and you are somewhere else, and it is all right, yet we both know . . .

It isn't.

You slide down the wooden door as August knocks again,

and again,

and again,

but he doesn't pound as loudly as my heart.

Funny, how hearts beat, wild and frantic, even in a ghost like me.

6

Momma,

I stare at you.

You are wearing your work uniform, but your shift should have started hours ago. You have never missed a day of work since you were hired at the grocery store as a cashier a few years back. But you are slumped against the door, hands clenched at your temples. You don't have makeup on either.

You always brush on your mask so the black and blue is buried under piles of CoverGirl twenty-four-hour foundation. You paint on eye shadow and blush, and your face always looks like a Crayola box. Fake.

I used to be embarrassed that you were my momma.

Embarrassed by how you smiled so much, lied so much with foundation and liner crinkling and smudging by your eyes. Yet, even in my embarrassment, I felt ashamed because I knew the pain hiding behind that mask.

Now here you are, face clean of makeup, eyes nearly swollen shut, the skin black and blue, not the powder. I walk closer to you and kneel down. I don't know if I imagine the cold floor or actually feel it.

I am not sure why I am taken aback, but I am. Without the makeup, without the lies, you look just like me.

Pale skin. Freckles. Chocolate eyes.

And like a quivering breath, a whisper of a vision at first, a memory shudders into place.

* * *

We have chocolate eyes.

It had been so long ago, but now I remember.

I was four, wasn't I?

I remember looking into the rearview mirror and seeing your eyes and saying, "Mommy, Mommy! We have the same color eyes!"

You beamed back at me. "Yes, we do, love. Chocolate! We have yummy chocolate eyes!" I liked that. Chocolate eyes. You had a long drawl to your voice. There was no twang to it, just a richness that made me think of sweet tea on summer days. I was still smiling when we pulled up to our house and saw an old '79 Cadillac in our driveway.

Your smile fell and you drove by our house.

"Mommy! You missed our house, silly!" I was giggling. I saw how you tensed up, the way you kept looking into the mirror, the way you drove to all the wrong places. We parked in parking lots and drove around neighborhood streets. You even stopped in front of a police station. I could hear your breathing. It was shaky. I asked you why we couldn't go home.

You didn't say anything at first. You just sat there staring out the window, looking like the only thing on your mind was *escape*. Then, the world came back into focus and you said, "Mommy's just thinking, sweetheart."

We sat in front of the police station a long time. You never got out of the car, and as the sun started to set, you pulled out of the parking spot and kept driving.

I didn't mind. I liked our drives. I stared out the window and thought of sweet, melting chocolate.

It was dark by the time we finally pulled up behind the Cadillac.

You looked in the rearview mirror. Your eyes were wet. "Hey, my girl. No matter what happens, it's you and me, okay? I'll keep you safe." Your voice shook. It didn't sound like a promise you could keep, but I believed you anyway.

I was wrong.

You did everything so slowly. The way you let the seat belt click before you started pulling it back. The way you turned toward your open door and let your feet hang before hopping down. The way you undid my booster seat belt and hugged me so tight. "Mommy, why are you crying?" I asked.

And you said, "Mommy just loves you so much, love."

You tried to carry me up the driveway, but I wiggled free, announcing that I was a big girl and wanted to walk. So you let me. You held my hand. It was so small. You kissed my fingertips and we walked to the door. It opened from the inside and I stared up at the man who stood on the threshold. His hair was black with a dusting of grey around his temples, his face scruffy. I hadn't seen him before.

"Mommy, who is that man in our house?" I asked you.

"Your father," you said, voice breaking. "That's your father, Ellie. And it looks like he found us."

He. Found. Us.

* * *

That was years ago. A memory dislodged.

The recall of that moment, once in place, was a solid and vivid thing. It blotted out the present for few seconds, as if it demanded every ounce of my attention. As if it mattered.

I exhale. I wish I could've gotten lost in it. I wish I could go back and live in those carefree days before he showed up at our door, but it is just a memory and nothing more. But maybe, just maybe, I will remember enough to know why. Why a piece of me, of my consciousness, was left *behind*. And maybe if I know why, I will know what I have to do to be gone from this limbo. Maybe the key is to understand.

I squeeze my eyes shut, probing for another moment, but no more memories come. I grit my teeth, desperate.

Please. Please. Please. Give me something more to hold on to. But Memory is cruel and keeps her secrets.

You move and I open my eyes. I realize the knocking has stopped. August must've left. Part of me wishes he would come back just so I could look at him again. But you move, and for a split second, it seems like you can see me. You are squeezing your arms around your legs. "I'm sorry. Oh, my dove, I am sorry. It's my fault," you say so softly.

I want to shake you. Of course it was. Of course it was your fault! Then I remember how you had said "he found us."

You whisper, "I was so close, so close."

I sit back on my invisible, ghostly self and stare at you. *So close? To what?*

I keep staring, waiting for you to answer. You don't. I cock my head to one side to examine you.

You are bruised, makeup-less, pale, with freckles and a split lip.

Under it all, I see the same woman who looked at me in the rearview mirror all those years ago, before we had a Cadillac parked in our driveway.

I see my momma who had chocolate eyes like mine.

You were so beautiful.

I look at my hands and think of how tightly you held on to them, how they hurt even as you planted kisses on my pudgy knuckles.

A realization hits: You died every day that you walked into this house.

Maybe you were a ghost long before I was.

A feeling that isn't anger pokes a hole in me and reaches out to you. I try to plug it up and push it down, push it away.

Because it hurts too much to know that now you are crying and it's because of me.

I reach out . . .

You jerk your head toward the door. The roar of an engine pulling in. That goddamned '76 Cadillac. You scurry to your feet and bolt up the stairs to the bathroom. Scrubbing your face with one hand, you reach with the other to pull out the bag of cheap makeup from under the cabinet. You have to paint your mask back on . . . otherwise, he will break you into little pieces until not even your fake doll face is left.

The face without freckles.

The face that looks nothing like mine.

7

Father,

I am staring out the window, watching you get out of your car. You pause for a second and look toward the street. I am a cannon and I want to blast right through you. Momma's in the bathroom and I am heading to our front door. The same doorway where I saw you for the first time all those years ago. I remember . . .

You hadn't always been cruel. That's what Momma told me once. That's what I vaguely remember from before the belts and whiskey bottles. Everything about the outside of you has stayed the same. The same wiry, strong build and flexing forearms, the same dark hair with shocks of gray, the same hooded eyes with crow's feet wrinkles that imply you smile often. You do, but most of those smiles are lies. The outside of you looks like the same man who stood on our porch all those years ago.

But it is your insides that have changed. They twisted up in your gut when no one was watching. Your voice sounds rough and low, but there was a time when I wasn't afraid of it. When I thought it sounded like a lullaby. You never sang, but the sound of it, the roll of it, lulled me to sleep.

When Momma held my hand so tight that it hurt as we walked up the driveway, you looked at us with eyes that made me think of a lost puppy we had found on the side of the road when we first moved into the row house on Sunset. It even had slick black fur and white patches. I wanted to keep it. Momma pulled over. It was raining and one of our windshield wipers wasn't working right so it was hard to see. She got out, took off her jacket, and wrapped up the little pup in it and then handed him to me to snuggle. He was small. So was I, and he didn't quite fit in my arms, but he nuzzled my neck and licked me. It tickled and we brought him home and I was laughing and coming up with names as we drove.

We had him for months. He peed on the floor. He chewed on Momma's shoes. He barked at squirrels. He was loud and messy and I loved him. But then one day, I had my arm dangling over the bed and when I heard his paws scratch on the hardwood, I smiled and smothered my face in a pillow. I knew he'd come and lick my fingertips like he usually did, but that day something was different.

He growled.

I started lifting my head from my pillow, eyebrows raised, but before I could say his name, he charged and clamped his jaw down on my forearm. The teeth dug in and a moment of shock gave way to pain as I tried to shake him off. He didn't let go. He was saliva and teeth and growls, and I screamed.

Momma yelled my name and I heard her frantic footsteps up the stairs. I begged him to let go, I tugged and pulled my arm, but it just made the pain worse. Momma lunged for us and she pried the dog's jaw open and I snatched my arm away the second it was loose. Momma wrestled with the dog until she could shove him outside and close the door. He growled at the door and barked through the wood.

"It hurts! It hurts!" I cried as Momma gathered me in her arms. Blood was everywhere. On my shirt. On my sheets. She scooped me up and then ran for the door. The dog kept barking and seemed poised to nip at her feet. We were out of the house. In the car. And on our way to the hospital. It was the first hospital visit I remember. It was the only hospital visit we didn't lie at during the intake.

No, this was before you. So there were no mysterious falls. Or bumped foreheads. Or accidents. Which were really all code for *Father Hurt Us Again*. This time it was just us and a dog's bite. I got ten stitches and when we came home, the growling mess of a dog, the dog I still loved even though it hurt me, was sent to a no-kill shelter.

When I looked at you standing on our front porch, I saw those sad-puppy eyes that I had snuggled on a car ride. You looked at Momma as if you could hardly believe she was real. You looked at me the same way. And you knelt down to cup my cheeks in your hands and told me that I was beautiful just like her, but even while you said it, you looked sad.

I still wanted to keep you.

I didn't know then that you'd bite too.

8

August,

The memory releases me from its grip. I inhale, breathing in the details, the familiarity of the moment without it settling properly in its place. Like a single piece of a thousand-piece jigsaw puzzle.

I need all of the pieces. How else will I be complete? How else will I be able to find my way?

Momma is still upstairs in the bathroom. I am still staring out our front door. Father is still in the driveway.

But it isn't until I look past my father, toward where his gaze is fixed near the sidewalk, that I see you. He's twirling his keys around his finger and looks like he is debating which direction to step in. I'm down the stairs and in the yard in a heartbeat. I want to put the entire population of our town between you, but there is just me and I am just air.

Father steps in your direction. "You're Ellie's friend, right?" His stride is lazy, his voice is soft.

August, you are standing on the sidewalk and your chest is heaving in breaths as you are clenching and unclenching your fists. "Yes," you say, quiet. Then louder, "Yes, I am."

Father nods, face solemn. Concerned.

I swallow. This feels like a trap.

"Sorry, young man. This is a shock to all of us. You should see Ellie's mother. Poor thing is devastated."

You don't say anything at first. Then carefully you say, "I am sorry for your loss, Mr. Walker."

Another slow and solemn nod. Father's hair is slicked back with sweat. He has a strong jaw, a crooked nose, and eyes as dark as the night sky. I used to be afraid of the dark, as if I thought I would see his eyes in it.

According to the ladies in town, Father was handsome. He was charming. He smiled and winked and pulled everyone under his spell, under his lies. No one knew what happened in our house on Sunset Street.

No one could believe that the man who spent his life building things out in the construction yard could come home to break things. But he did. And he did it with a smile.

Father looks like he is about to turn toward the house,

but steps in August's direction again as if remembering something.

"She was out with you, wasn't she? The night before last? A couple nights before *it* happened?"

I blink. We had been together? Recently? The confusion tugs at me in different directions. I can't even remember two days ago.

You look startled. Uneasy. You shift from foot to foot.

"Ah, maybe it wasn't you, then. She came home and cried her eyes out. Poor thing. Some are just built that way, you know." Father sighed. "Hmm, I wonder if . . ." Then he waved it off as if whatever idea had popped into his head was ridiculous, and turned toward the house.

"Wonder if what?" You take a step forward, suddenly alert.

"Oh, you know, if whatever happened that night made her . . ." Father's voice trails off. He doesn't need to finish the thought. The shock that settles onto your face is telling enough. I had been with you. It is plain on your face, but I can't remember it.

"I guess we will never know," Father says as he turns toward the house.

The edge of his lip curls up in a cruel smirk. I am the only one who sees it.

My father doesn't only deal pain out in bruises. He knows just the words to say to make you feel unsteady. Like you're falling.

But what happened two nights ago? I had never gone out before. I went to sleep every night with my door locked and a pillow braced over my head so I couldn't hear the groans down the hall.

I look at you. Your eyes are wet and you are shaking.

Your eyes are so big that I think your tears could drown the world.

I remember the day that you, August Matthews, came into my life.

* * *

It was the first day of kindergarten. You were kind of funny-looking when I first met you. I remember thinking that your head was a size too big for your body and your eyes were as big as the saucer dishes that we used to put milk in for the stray cats in our neighborhood.

Before I started school, I was comfortable being with Momma all the time, and now I was one bobbing head in a sea of others. I was one of the smaller ones and I found myself looking up all the time. I looked at everyone and wondered who would share their crayons with me. I scanned my eyes around the room, trying to pick out who I thought would be nice and who I should avoid. Your face appeared out of nowhere and you stood too close.

"Hi! I am August Matthews." You weren't that much taller than me. "I like your backpack."

It was a Power Rangers backpack. I didn't want the

girly pink one. I liked the Red Ranger because he seemed the strongest.

A bigger kid knocked into me and I fell down. It hurt my palms and I wanted to cry, but I didn't. I felt a little hand on my shoulder. "Are you okay?"

"Yeah, I am okay."

You helped me up. "You are so clumsy, Jeffrey! You can't push people! I will tell on you to Ms. Lindsay!" you said as you puffed out your chest and glared at the boy with a shock of yellow hair and a scowl on his face. He was bigger than both of us, but still you glared at him with your saucer eyes. I felt scared of him, but the way you stood, seemingly unafraid, made me stand straighter too. The older boy rolled his eyes and started to march toward the school's front doors.

"Thanks," I said.

You seemed confused for a second when you looked at my backpack. "Do you have everything for class?" You must have noticed how flat it was. I hadn't bought any of the supplies. "I'll be okay. I just need crayons."

Your saucer eyes lit up again. "Oh!" You pulled your backpack off your shoulder and unzipped it. "You can have some of mine. I have extra. I like to color."

You were smiling, and so, as the teachers shuffled us into different lines, I opened my backpack and stuffed the box of crayons inside. I saw the front and my jaw dropped. "They have sparkles in them!"

You laughed. "Draw a unicorn!" you shouted, as the lines were pulling us apart.

"I don't know how!" I shouted back.

"Then I'll draw you one!"

And the next day, when we saw each other before getting sorted into our different classes, you handed me a drawing of a beautiful unicorn and rainbow, complete with shimmery crayon. I squealed with delight and you laughed. You laughed a lot.

You laughed wholeheartedly and loud.

And I liked it.

* * *

You aren't laughing now. You are hunched over and look too old and too young all at the same time. Father doesn't see as you clench and unclench your fists with his back turned. When he slams our front door shut, you stand up tall, all six-feet and one-inch of you, and run.

You run so fast. Faster than I remember when we were kids. Your feet pound the pavement and your messenger bag is flying off your shoulder. It is a long run to your house, but I am right there beside you, pretending that we are ten years old and racing to our own hiding place in the woods where we would build worlds and rule them.

Your home is blue like the sky and you have shutters that are red like blood. I remember telling you that once and you didn't like it very much. You fly up your steps and fling open your front door. It is just as beautiful as I remember it inside. Crisp, beige paint on the walls with perfect white crown-molding. Hardwood floors that look like they are cloaked in honey.

Your mother sets her cup on the table and looks up at you from the kitchen. She is older than my momma. Wrinkles at the corners of her eyes. She's not wearing doll makeup. There aren't bruises on her skin. She's older, but she isn't used up.

Her eyes are wide with concern. "August, what's wrong, baby?"

You stare at her from the doorway, chest heaving in breaths, huge, heavy breaths.

"She's . . . She's . . . dead."

Your mom squints her eyes as if it can help her hear. Your voice is so soft.

"She's dead," you say louder, angrier.

She stands up suddenly and is walking toward you, worry in her eyes. "Who? Who is dead? What are you talking about?"

"Ellie." I see it in the tremble of your lip and the way you swallow hard. The tension bunches your shoulders; the tears are caught somewhere in your eyes, but you won't let them out.

I don't think I have ever seen you cry.

I don't think I want to.

I don't think I can.

I start to back away, to run from the wave of emotion

that I feel is about to crash against the Matthews' house, and as I step over the threshold, it happens.

Your mom gathers you into her arms and you bury your head in her shoulder. It is strange to see someone so large needing to collapse on someone so small. I turn to run, but I hear your muffled shaky voice, "She's dead. She's dead. She's dead."

The tide has washed me in and I can't leave.

I don't know how long you cling to your mom, but I know she isn't the one to let go.

* * *

Now you are in the middle of your room, sitting in one of those rotating chairs, and you swing slowly around, over and over again. I have never been in your room. It almost feels wrong to be here now. . . .

You stop turning finally. I am sitting on your bed. The blankets look soft. Your walls are plastered with posters. Posters of bands, T-shirts, and sketches. I remember you used to invite me to concerts. I remember always saying no.

I don't notice the two small photos that are tacked up between the glossy designed posters until you stand up to touch them.

One is a picture of the inside of the red barn bridge. *Our* red barn bridge. The one below it is me. Not me from years ago when we played in our little cove of trees and when you carried a Walmart disposable camera around. But me, from one year ago. I don't know how or when you took it, but you did.

I was sitting at a picnic table. It was a school day; we were released early. I hadn't wanted to go home yet so I went to the park. How did I not see you there? Watching? Following? Why didn't you say anything?

I had taken out my notebook and started to scribble in the corners in my strange way. I didn't like to write on the ruled lines until the words came, the right words. I curled my script down margins and used arrows to point at good ideas. I must've found a good one, because there in the picture I sat, pencil in hand, staring at the page, and I was smiling.

I don't know what it was that I thought or read. I don't know how I didn't hold on to it and treasure it, because looking at the photo, my eyes alight with something like satisfaction, my lips quirked up so much that my eyes were almost squinty, I was . . .

I can't say the word or think it without my stomach twisting.

Beautiful.

Maybe it was how you took the picture, how the light hit my face in a brilliant golden way, how my freckles somehow made my face look happier.

I don't know what magic you used to make it so. I wish I had seen the picture before. I wish I had known what I could look like. What I could be.

I wish I had known what you saw when you looked at me.

Your eyes are red. You trace your fingers over the photo-graph. Reverence, sweetness.

I know what those fingers feel like.

The truth of that shocks me, because here in your room, I can't remember. I can't remember when you would've touched me or why, but when I look at your hands, I know they are gentle. I know that even though they are precise with a pen, they are hesitant on skin.

I swallow hard and wish I could feel them now.

Your slender fingers pause and curl around the edges of the photo. Your jaw clenches and rage flickers across your face. You crumple the photo in your palm. You turn around and fling it against the opposite wall. I stand bolt upright and stare at the place where it falls on the ground. I don't see when you pick up your chair, but I hear it as it slams against the drywall. I flinch at the crashing sound. I cover my ears as if it could rupture my eardrums. Your guitar is in your hands and you swing it like a bat and it pounds and pounds and pounds into your headboard and then your desk and then the wall.

Nothing is safe. I look over your room, filled with draw-ings, trinkets, family photos, and I want to save them all. You have snow globes from all over the world and I lunge to cover them, but I am just air and the guitar smashes into them. Your face, it isn't yours. It is someone else's. Someone who is hard and cruel, broken and merciless and . . .

Did I ruin you? The thought slams into me.

"August!" I yell your name, aching and desperate for you to stop. But you don't hear me. Of course you don't.

You let go of the guitar. Your mom is calling your name and you run to lock the door. You nearly trip over the fallen objects. Switching the lock on, you rest your head on the door and your palm splays beside it. You are shaking. Gritting your teeth, tears find their way out of your scrunched-up eyes. You are turning red and I am afraid you will explode.

"I'm sorry. I'm sorry. I'm sorry." You are crying and shaking and I want to take the hurt away.

You pound the wall with your fist. Turning around, your back is up against the door.

Your mom is pounding on it from the other side, yelling your name.

You don't respond. Your apologies turn into questions. "Why?" You say it over and over again, as if in prayer, as if there is someone who could tell you.

Whywhywhywhy. The question reverberates down to my bones like an accusation. I should know. I want to cup your cheeks and tell you the truth. The truth I don't know, but wish I could remember.

Still, I know in my hollow bones it was never your fault. My August boy of sunshine, lightning bugs, and birthdays.

You finally stop speaking and shuffle onto your knees and crawl to the spot where the crumbled photograph lies on the ground.

You pick it up and fervently uncrumple it and nestle it in your cut, bloody hands.

"Why?" you ask again. "Why?" Your fingers are feather-light again, stroking my cheek as if you could push the wisps of my hair behind my ear. As if I am there.

You finally whisper my name and it is the saddest word in the world.

9

Momma,

I stay with August until he falls asleep amid his wreckage, until his momma finally pries open his bedroom door. Her eyes are red and she sharply inhales when she sees her son asleep among shards of glass. She doesn't wake him. Her heels crunch over the brokenness and she slides down the wall beside him in her knee-length pencil skirt. I don't know if the glass cuts her, because the tears are streaming down her face even before she hits the ground. August doesn't wake. Grief seems like a heavy and exhausting burden to bear. Mrs. Matthews just holds August close and then closer, as if she is afraid that if she lets him go, he would disappear.

That's when I leave.

Tears in the wake behind me.

I don't run home. I walk. I am in no rush. I thought I was lonely when I was alive, but being dead is pretty damn lonely.

I look at my bare feet. I miss my inked-up Converse shoes. They had quotes from my favorite authors Sharpied all over them. I remember finding them in a thrift store bin when I was twelve. They were too big for me at the time, but I already knew I wanted to be a writer. So anytime I read a line that took my breath away or stumbled on a quote that made me believe in big and wonderful things, I would write them on my shoes. *These shoes will carry me through this ugly world*, I had thought. And when I was fifteen and the shoes were still a bit too big but fit well enough, I started to wear them every day.

I am back in my room. I wish I could sleep, tuck the questions away, but time feels disjointed and too long. The moon is ripe and full in the sky. There is so much missing in my mind. So much that I feel is swimming just under the surface.

I don't look at the chair or metal bowl of ash in the corner. Looking haunts me. I stare out the window trying to remember. Father is snoring in the next room. I toss the memories that came to me back and forth. Is the only way forward, the only way out of this limbo, to look back? But for what purpose?

I sit and think. Analyze. So far, the memories have been chronological, and each came to me in the present while watching the person at the center of that experience. If the memories continued that way, maybe I just need to keep probing, keep pushing until all of them spill out in order. Like a tether to the truth that I could follow. Maybe once I know, I can move on.

I hear a sound and realize it is you. Momma, your whimpers are choked and smothered by a pillow. August was held by his mother when he cried, but there is no one here to hold you.

I remember smothering my tears with a pillow too. I go to you. I see the tangles in your hair and I want to brush my fingers through them. I want to clean up your grief because it makes me uncomfortable, it makes me feel worse. I want to scrub you clean. Head to toe. I want to shove all your tears into a corner and lock them up so I can look at you without my chest aching.

But then I think of how you looked like someone who didn't quite fit in the small space of her kitchen, in the cramped sliver of her life, and I wonder if I was one of the people who pushed you there. I sit back on my heels.

No.

No, Father chipped your crown away. Your chocolate-brown eyes open and I will myself to look deeply into them. *Tell me,* I whisper. This time without accusation. This time just to see.

To see you and how you changed from the woman I recognized in the rearview mirror, bright smiles and laughter, to the woman who no longer fit into her life. Maybe that will help me understand why I could no longer fit in my own.

And as if I pushed on a door, it opens and I see a thread of memories that tells me not enough and too much at the same time.

* * *

You hadn't always worked at the grocery store. Before the Dixie's red apron and uniform, I remember you having clothes that made you look smart and fancy. I think you worked in an office. You even had a briefcase with papers inside. You'd pick me up from school in your minivan and squish me in a big mommy hug and then we'd hold hands when we got home and march up our driveway. Your heels click-click-clicked on the floor. My light-up-sole tennis shoes sort of squished instead of clicked.

"How was your day, love?" you'd ask.

And I yammered on about August and his drawings or my kindergarten teacher's bug collection or our classroom's pet rabbit or learning how the letters of words fit together. You'd listen and make excited faces on cue. As I talked, you'd kick off your heels and rub your feet and set me up at the kitchen table to color or do homework, and then you'd start cooking.

When Father first moved in, our routine didn't change. He'd just come home from work and somehow slide into the flow of it. A baritone addition to our kitchen. He'd lean against the countertop and ask you what you were cooking. He'd kiss your neck. He'd toss a "Good job, kid" in my direction when I displayed my coloring masterpiece. He fit. He took up space but didn't dominate it.

You didn't smile much at first. You'd watch him carefully, studying him as if you weren't sure you could see him quite right. But as the seasons changed and our flow continued, you started to laugh when he joked, or smile when he wrapped his arms around you in the kitchen. You stopped stiffening every time he'd sit with me.

Father was a head taller than you. You fit just under his chin when he hugged you, and just like he seemed to fit right in our kitchen and lives, you seemed to fit there with him. His shoulders were broader, his arms longer, and he wrapped you up and you'd close your eyes and breathe him in.

One day, as you were frying chicken and the oil popped and crackled, Father came in with his booming voice and said, "How are my girls doin'?" Arms outstretched in the kitchen doorway. I lunged out of my chair and got to him first. It was a race to see who got the first hug. He knelt down to squeeze me and then he let me go and I ran back to the table to try to draw a copy of a picture that August had given me: a cheetah in the jungle.

My drawings never looked like August's. Eventually, I

stopped trying to redraw them and instead I'd make up stories that I'd tell him the next day. But that day, I was still trying to retrace his steps and perfect spots that looked more like globs on my too-short, too-squished cheetah. Father looked at you and cocked his head. "Hmmm . . ." he said. It was a sound he'd make when something smelled good in the kitchen or when he pulled you into his chest for a kiss.

You smiled. Your hair was pulled into a messy bun with a pen. You were turning the chicken in the pan and looked over at him when he didn't move. "What?"

My gaze went back to my page. I was coloring and searching for a different orange. I knew the shade. Sunset. Just like our street name.

"I never noticed how short your work skirts are."

"My . . . skirts?" You chuckled. "They practically touch my knees. They aren't short at all."

There was teasing in his voice. "Those knees must make the men wild." I wasn't looking, but I knew that Father was wrapping his arms around you. His voice was closer. Sort of muffled as he kissed the back of your head. It's funny how we can hear so much. A movement. A gesture. A feeling in a voice, a sound.

Like I knew that you threw your head back when you laughed even though I didn't see it, because the laugh was so sudden and loud. That's what you used to do when a laugh took you by surprise. "Oh, stop it."

That night, he did.

We went on with our flow. Our routine. But little things started to change. Subtle things.

You'd ask if I had seen a skirt. You'd search for a pair of heels. Father would drink in the scent of you when he got home and then ask why you smelled of cologne, which made you blink in response. You'd sniff yourself and say, "I don't know what you are talking about, babe." And you'd offer your wrist for inspection. I thought you smelled of strawberries.

He'd ask why you were smiling for seemingly no reason and that made you laugh. Not in a head-thrown-back way, but in a tight way, like you had to stuff it between you as a buffer. He started talking about how late dinner was and how hungry he was and how his momma had dinner ready when his poppa walked in the door. All of this was tucked into hugs, and kisses, and surprise flowers, and our nightly flow.

I barely noticed how you started to go straight into the kitchen to cook rather than swing my hand as we talked about my day. Or how you started checking the clock. Or how I knew I shouldn't talk so much once he sat at the table because he just wanted some quiet. Little things. He'd fit into our flow, but just like a boulder can shift the waters around it, Father did too. At first, we didn't see how our current was disrupted.

One day, your car didn't start. It was an old car. It wasn't surprising. I was in the back seat and you hit the steering wheel in frustration. You sighed. "Well, love, looks like we are going to walk to school today."

"Let's go!" I gathered my book bag and slid off my booster seat. We walked to school, swinging hands.

"Aren't you going to be late to work?"

"Yeah, I'll be late. But it should be okay. I'll just bring some work home with me to finish up. And your father used to work in a mechanic shop, so he should know what's wrong with the car. I'll call him when I get home and then call a taxi to take me to work."

We didn't walk home from school at the end of that day. You picked me up and waved to me from the back of Mr. Grayson's bright green sedan. "Look, Ellie! We got a ride."

We didn't have taxis in our town. It was too small for that. But Mr. Grayson was retired and had a new shiny car and was only a phone call away if anyone needed a ride. He had four Black Ice car freshener trees hanging off the rear-view mirror and I loved the smell of them. I felt like we were from those movies with rich people who had drivers. The seats were black and smooth and the windows were electric. I played with the control, watching them go up and down. You laughed.

When we got home, you paid Mr. Grayson and he tipped his hat to both of us with a furry, bearded "Enjoy yer day, m'ladies!"

Your car wasn't in the driveway. "I guess your father already brought it to the shop. . . ."

And sure enough, when we walked through the door, Father was already washing his hands in the kitchen. There was black stuff on them. He looked up. "My girls!" He smiled. And we went to hug him, his hands still under the stream of faucet water.

"Did you take the car to the shop already?"

He paused washing, but didn't look at you. "Yep. Should be done this weekend."

Relief melted your expression. "Oh, good. Mr. Grayson is a godsend, but I won't be able to pay for rides for too long." You took off your heels and set them by the door.

But the car wasn't ready by that weekend.

Or the next.

When you voiced your frustration, he teetered from "It will be ready soon" to "You shouldn't have to work" to "Don't you trust me to take care of you?" Dinners started to feel tense and the kitchen started feeling too small and I started to bring my coloring up to my room. I could feel the shift. The current change.

And then one day, all of your work clothes were gone.

Everything.

No heels.

No skirts.

No blouses.

You erupted. When Father walked through the door, you yelled at him. He didn't move. He just listened, his face deathly calm. Then he told you he had sold the clothes. He said he'd sold the car because he couldn't fix it and you didn't have enough money to keep it at the shop. That it didn't make sense for you to keep working.

You slapped your hands against the countertops. "That is not a decision that you can make!"

And then Father cocked his head and narrowed his eyes. His back was straight and he walked slowly toward where you stood. "Everything that happens in this house is my decision," he said, his breath on your cheek. It almost sounded like a teasing whisper. But it wasn't.

It was a growl.

Your eyes changed then. You searched his face and suddenly recognition lit your eyes. I hadn't seen this man before, but you had. And that's what you'd been looking for all those months, that's who you were trying to see, but then you forgot that he was there. You forgot to look. But then you saw.

You didn't shout. Your voice matched his low, dusky quiet. "I think—you should leave."

"You think . . . I should leave. Let me tell you what I think . . ." His fingers grazed up your arm, up your throat, and then his one, two, three, four fingers wrapped around your neck and squeezed. Your hands fumbled at his as you tried to pry his hand away. "I think you should be a good girl and listen." He whispered in your ear and then he let go. You rattled out a cough. "Shhh, shhh, shhh." He wrapped you up in a hug and tried to lull you back into quiet, back into

53

him. He was soft and tender as he rocked you in his arms. Like he was trying to rock you to sleep. But I saw your eyes.

They were wide open.

Father's cruelty bit when we least expected it. Between movie nights and Saturday pancakes. His laugh bellowed in our home, but there were times when we'd have to tiptoe around his mood, afraid to set it off like a bomb. It only got worse with time, when whiskey started getting stockpiled on our pantry shelves. Your smiles and laughter started sounding hollow and when you looked at him as he walked in the door, you would hug and kiss him, but the moment you turned away, your face fell.

Our home was a little run-down. Peeling paint, old laminate countertops, cabinets with caving-in bottoms, sofas that had holes, and flowers that looked like they were drooping. There was a time when none of that mattered; it was home. But as the years passed, the house felt like it was crumbling from the inside out, just like our fake smiles.

While life had been changing for a while, it snapped into a before-and-after with the sound of a slap.

On the way home one day, you had asked me, "Ellie, wouldn't it be amazing to see the mountains right outside of our window?" You were looking at our neighborhood as if seeing more than the boarded-up doors, barred windows, and rusty playground equipment in abandoned yards.

I loved the mountains. I loved the way my chest and my legs ached as we climbed up trails, and the peaks where it looked like we could see the whole world while sitting cross-legged with peanut butter and jellies. But I looked at our neighborhood and couldn't see beyond the rust and dried grass. I couldn't see whatever wondrous thing you had built up before your eyes. "There are no mountains around here, Momma."

You were quiet for a moment before looking ahead toward our driveway. "You are right. There are no mountains here. But what if we chased them?" You looked at me then, a smile flickering across your lips.

"I'd like that! An adventure."

"That's right, beautiful. Our own little adventure."

We didn't say anything else as we climbed the stairs. Father was inside.

I ran to Father for a hug that felt too tight and my chest felt compressed with too little air. "Father! We are going to chase the mountains!" I squealed. I was practically bouncing in his lap with excitement.

His eyebrows pitched up. "Oh really? And how are we gonna chase the mountains, doll?"

"We are going to go on an adventure, silly. We could drive . . ."

"Momma doesn't have a car . . ."

"We could fly! Or walk! I am a very good walker." I puffed out my chest. I knew I would be the best adventurer.

"And whose idea was it to go on this little adventure?"

"Momma's!"

"Ellie . . ." Your voice was soft yet urgent, but I was too excited to pay attention.

"She said that we could live in a house and have mountains right outside our windows and . . ."

"Is that so?" Father said.

"Ellie . . . ," you said at the same time.

I was thinking about treasure maps and big windows and mountain peaks. I didn't notice the air getting sucked out of the room or the way you and Father watched each other. On a razor's edge. A step away from explosive mines in the floorboards that I was too oblivious to see.

"Go upstairs, Ellie," Father said.

I ran upstairs, skipping steps and humming all the way to my room. My bedroom floor vent looked into the kitchen and I perched myself above it and spied. I couldn't see everything. But I could see enough.

You and Father didn't move from your spots. You stared at each other. I had thought that you'd both be excited, but something was taut between you and I suddenly felt all wrong. My tapping toes and humming stopped.

"The mountains, huh?"

"Abel, we were just daydreaming. You know, make-believe as we walked home."

Father reached for the glass of whiskey that I hadn't seen on the table and took a long sip until it was empty.

I looked at you and your eyes were squeezed shut.

Father stood up, his chair croaking as it slid across the floor.

The slap was like a thunderclap.

Father was looming over you. You were holding your cheek. Your shoulders were heaving in little breaths and then your eyes flicked up to the ceiling and found mine through the vent. I started to get to my knees so I could run downstairs to see if you were okay, but with the slightest shake of your head I knew that I had to stay where I was. I had to just watch and do nothing. I held my breath.

Father grabbed a fistful of your hair and then nuzzled your neck. "Don't think I don't know who you are, Regina. You left me once. You won't leave me again." You closed your eyes and gave a tiny nod. His voice went lower. "If you try, Regina, I swear, if you try to chase mountains or chase daydreams . . . I will chase you. I will find you. And you will regret stepping out of this house."

Then he kissed you, only to break away to say, "You are mine and you aren't going anywhere."

And we didn't.

That was the first day you wore your doll face.

The violence snuck into our home slowly and all I could do was look away and hide.

A grab. A slap. A shove against the wall.

He'd beat you and then when you were done hiccupping tears in the bathroom with the shower running so no one could hear you, he'd come back and stroke your hair. He'd whisper apologies and nuzzle your neck. He'd make promises that he'd never keep and you sniffled and still let him make them just so he would stroke your hair a little longer.

It is easy to give yourself away. You do it little by little until you are left with nothing but your bones in your hands and you wonder how so much was taken without you noticing. You painted on a face to pretend. You painted on a face so you didn't have to see the lies looking back at you.

"Momma, why can't we leave?" I asked one night from under my covers. You had been stroking my hair.

You paused your stroking and took in a deep breath. "We will, one day. I promise." Your voice was a whisper and when you saw the look on my face, you kept speaking in hushed tones. "When I first met your father, I fell in love with him. I never thought he would hurt me. But then, when I got pregnant with you . . . he changed. He was violent. He was . . . controlling. He scared me and I ran away. But I didn't know he'd chase me. Chase us. Wherever we went, he was always just a few steps behind. And when he finally found us here, he seemed to have changed. I was wrong. So wrong. But when we leave, we have to be ready. We have to be able to go far, far away. I am afraid of what he might do if he finds us the next time."

* * *

I am knocked back. The thread of memories tangles up around my heart and tugs so tight I feel like it leaves cuts. I can't feel your cheek now, but I remember falling asleep as you stroked mine that same night. The night of the promise in the dark.

It was just a lullaby to soothe me, but as you fall asleep now, hiccupping little breaths, there is no one here to soothe you. I hear my bedroom door creak and Father is there. I want to rush him, beat my hands against his chest, but he just walks over to my bed and scoops you up into his arms and carries you back down the hall to your bedroom.

You either don't wake up or pretend to still be asleep.

Pain had followed us like a shadow.

And now I am following my life like one too.

10

Words,

I remember now when I first believed that I could change our lives—it was because of you.

You didn't always fit easily in my mouth. When I was younger, I would fumble with your letters and mispronounce your syllables. I slammed a book shut in second grade because of my white-hot frustration when I tried to read you. I had been in the school library for mandatory reading time. It was the worst hour of the school day and I resented feeling stupid and lacking.

The librarian saw my aggression toward one of her beloved books and came over and sat next to me. I thought she would scold me. She had a pinched face and a severe jaw-line that was perfectly made for reprimands. I braced myself.

Instead she tapped the book and whispered, "When I was little, it was hard for me to read."

"It was?" I hadn't expected that confession. I peered up at her. Her gaze was soft and open, her harsh features transformed into something almost lovely. She nodded.

"I always forgot the sounds the letters made when smooshed together and I hated books."

I blinked at her. "But—but you are a librarian."

"Yes, I am." She smiled. "Do you know why?"

I shook my head.

"Because I found out the secret about words."

"What's the secret?" I leaned in, waiting. Expectant.

She smiled, almost conspiratorially, and leaned in closer. "They are magic."

11

August,

The next day, I walk to your house, and as I stand outside, I know you are there. There is music drifting down from your open bedroom window. It is so much softer than anything I ever listened to. It feels like falling, like musical notes that could cry and break you down along with them.

I want to fall into your arms, August. I want all the memories that I can't grasp to hold me close and closer still. Just so I can understand. Because if I've been left behind with nothing but this slow trickle of memories to lead me forward, I know that our memories will give me solid ground to stand on.

I close my eyes and listen to the music, hearing you in it, the peace and quiet and gentleness. It takes me a moment to recognize the familiarity of it. I had drifted on these notes before. In a place that was for dreams and dreamers.

And then that's when I remember: I was the one who showed you the place. *Our* place.

* * *

We were seven. I had cut through Britney's yard and found it while trying to climb the tallest tree near the rows of houses. It was a small cove with purple flowers and low branches for climbing. There had been some fallen-over logs that looked like dugouts for war. It was perfect.

As soon as I laid eyes on it, I knew I wanted to take you there.

I held your skinny, callus-less hands and dragged you behind me. You had grown taller and you couldn't quite keep up with your limbs, so you kept tripping over every bit of underbrush. I laughed when you fell and you would give me your fake-glare every time.

"Hurry up!" I teased.

Your big saucer eyes didn't disappoint. The moment we stepped into the clearing, they grew five times wider. "Wow, Ellie! It's perfect."

I let go of your hand and ran to jump on a log. "I told you it would be!" I walked across the log, balancing with my arms outstretched. "This can be our secret place. We can rule it."

"As king and queen?" you said, turning slowly around the space, admiring it.

"No, as warriors." I lunged for you and pushed you down. "Ellie Walker takes down August Matthews with one—" My narration was interrupted as you pulled me down and sat on top of me, grabbing my fists to make me hit myself.

You took over the fight's narration. "Then Ellie, crazy from mutant poisoning, starts to hit herself in the—"

"Do your stories always have to include mutant poisoning?" I said, pushing as hard as I could so I wouldn't slap myself.

"Uh, only the best ones do."

I rolled my eyes. And hid a smile.

That little cove set behind the Fairfield subdivision and nestled in the woods became our sanctuary for years. It was also the first place that made me realize you could create a new world and live in it. You could shut out all the ugliness and the realness of everything else and laugh so loud that it hurt. I liked that pain. And there in our little sanctuary was the only place I felt it.

Shortly after that first day, you pinned me down by my shoulders and I flailed to wiggle free. "Is that all you got, Walker?" you asked. Your canine tooth was missing because you fell off the monkey bars and knocked it loose. It made you look adorable, disarming. I pulled my feet up to my chest and kicked. You plopped back into the dirt and moss at the base of the sycamore trees.

"I guess not."

You roared as you lunged forward to knock me over again. I faked left and then pivoted to my right and you fell to your knees in an inglorious and messy thud. Laughter erupted from me and you looked back over your shoulder to glare, but nothing you did was truly based in anger, although you sometimes did try to make a show of it. It didn't take long for your big mouth to quirk up in a grin. You were laughing by the time I stood up.

"Fine. We'll call this one a draw."

"A draw?" I scoffed, indicating that there was a clear victor in this round.

"Okay, fine. You win. A-E rules, right?"

"Right." I grinned. "A-E rules" was our code. You would continue wrestling me in the woods if, and only if, I wouldn't tell anyone when I won. It was our secret. We were super-heroes and warriors in these woods set between the river and the subdivision. I still liked playing with sticks and wielding them like swords. I was a fighter.

I looked up to the sky. The sun was starting to dip and I stiffened. "I have to go home."

"Oh, c'mon! We didn't get here till late today. Just stay out for another hour."

"I'll get in trouble."

"Don't be a wuss. What's the point if you don't get into trouble every now and then?"

I looked away from you toward a small creek. It was a skinny, spidery waterway that fed into the river. I knew the kind of trouble you were talking about. I saw when your mom would pull you aside, all pointy fingers and stern voice and say, "You're grounded for three days!" which really meant you were grounded for one. And even then, you could watch TV and have friends over. I wasn't really sure how that was a legitimate punishment for anything. I didn't resent you for it. I was a mix of envious and happy for you.

You didn't have to be home before seven o'clock so you could wash all the evidence off. You didn't have to go home and sit quietly at a table and feel the sweat drip down your spine because you wondered how many drinks your father had had.

"I'm going home," I said, and I didn't look back. I was sad and angry. I was scared to go home, but also mad that you thought I was a wuss.

"C'mon, Walker . . . just a few more."

I ran. I didn't want to be convinced. If I was late, he would hit Momma again. She still had a bruise from when I spilled milk two days before. It was yellow, black, and all unnatural skin colors. I thought that even the body knows when something is wrong and I didn't want to cause more wrong to blossom on her skin.

I ran faster when I heard you behind me trying to catch up. I rarely won when we wrestled, but I always won when we raced. I ran faster and faster until the subdivision came into view. I cut through the Percys' yard and leaped onto the pavement. I didn't glance back because I knew you weren't following me anymore. I couldn't hear your steps slow. You probably stopped at the tree line. Stopped at the threshold of our world of heroes and fantasy. You could stay there for a while longer.

I couldn't.

I was home on time. All washed up. Clean. Quiet. The air felt oppressive. The house felt cramped. Not a word. *Be a good girl*, I thought.

Later, Father was drinking his whiskey and I heard the growl of his voice and the hushed murmur of my momma's. Father shouting. I thought I heard my name, but I shoved my head under my pillow and tried not to hear. Momma didn't cry. I always did. I hoped that one day, I could learn how not to cry too. I took my hand and wiped my nose. It came away with a line of snot on it. I looked around for a tissue or paper towel. I didn't have one.

I wasn't going to the bathroom to get a tissue. I looked in my drawer and took out a mismatched sock and wiped it across my arm. I didn't get in my pj's. I slipped into my cocoon of a blanket and fell asleep.

The next morning, I went to my door to open it and narrowed my eyes when I realized it was locked. It only locked from the inside and I didn't lock it. Someone had reached in, turned the lock, and closed it behind them.

My momma had locked my door to keep me safe.

* * *

Our little sanctuary always kept us safe. It was where we both ran to escape, to play, to be free.

I remember I first started to tell stories there when we were ten.

You groaned as you entered our clearing. "I hate them!"

I didn't look up. "Hate who?"

You collapsed next to me, plopping right into a patch of wishing flowers, and I almost slapped your arm for ruining them before my gaze caught on how the seeds fluttered in the air and sunlight. Like little dreams with fluffy parachutes. I didn't blow the seeds free, but I closed my eyes and made a wish anyway.

"My parents!"

"You don't hate your parents."

"Yes, I do."

"Why?" I had met your parents. They wore ironed clothes and had gelled hair and smiles almost as big as yours (no one had a smile quite as big as yours). They called me Miss Ellie, as if I was already grown. I liked them.

"Because they are so old. And boring. And like, they just don't get me, you know?" You started to pick at a scab on your knee.

"Stop that." I smacked your hand away. You looked at me as if I had just slapped you square in the face. I rolled my eyes. "You'll scar if you keep picking." I knew all about scars. I didn't want to see any on you.

You huffed out a breath. "So I have been talking to them about these two things for weeks now and they just keep putting it off and I finally cornered them and told them to give me an answer and they flat-out said no. They knew all along they would say no and they just made me wait!"

I looked at the way your face scrunched up into angry lines. "What did they say no to?"

"They won't let me go to art camp this summer."

I sat up straighter. You had just won the art award at school. You had a collection of paintings hanging in our school hallway. Every single notebook you owned was framed in elaborate pencil drawings. You had been talking about going to the art camp in the city for two whole years. You were finally old enough.

Maybe I didn't like your parents either. "That's so stupid!"

"I know!"

Art camp would mean you would be away for six weeks in the summer. I bristled the first time you talked about it because I knew I would miss you. But I never wanted it taken away from you. You belonged there.

"We have to figure out a way for you to go."

"It's impossible. It costs nine hundred and fifty dollars. Where can I get money like that?"

This is where I would've liked to remember how we came up with some ingenious idea and the whole community rallied and then we said our sniffly farewells as you headed off to camp. That is the movie version. But we didn't live in the movies. I scooted closer to you and leaned my head on your shoulder. You were plucking the seeds off the flowers—pinching bunches, tearing them off, and tossing them in the grass beside you. It didn't look like you were making a wish. It looked like you were throwing it away.

"Tell me a story," you whispered.

This had become our game over the past few months. I would tell you stories and you would draw me promises. We wrote and drew our way out of our worst days. Sometimes I didn't understand your anger. Sometimes the things that wrecked your day seemed so small in comparison to the bruises on my back. But still, I wanted to take all of that hurt away, even if I didn't understand it, because it was yours and I didn't want it to be.

"There was a b—"

"No, start with 'Once upon a time.'"

"Why?"

"Isn't that how the fairy tales all start? That way we know it will be a happy ending."

Not all fairy tales have happy endings, but I didn't tell you that.

"Once upon a time," I began.

You closed your eyes to listen and I whispered a tale about a boy who painted things into reality. A drawn door that was a portal to anywhere. A painted star you could sit on and dip your toes into ocean sky. An acrylic wishing flower whose seeds could be ridden to what you desired most in the whole world. A magic boy with a paintbrush who was ridiculed until he showed the world what he could do.

You were smiling by the end. I was too. You opened up your eyes and searched the patches of grass around you. "What are you looking for?" I asked.

You tugged on one fluffy wishing flower.

"We will both get out of here, Ellie."

"We will both get out of here," I repeated, because sometimes you have to say things out loud even if you don't know if they can be true.

"Let's blow out this wishing flower together." Saucer eyes. Big smile. "If the fuzzy flowers fly away, then we'll know that our wish will come true."

I sat back. I didn't want to blow out the flower. I didn't want to squeeze my eyes shut and heave out a long breath only to open my eyes to see a cluster of seeds still stuck there, mocking me for dreaming too big. I'd had that happen before. I didn't want to know that the wish wouldn't come true. But you raised the flower in front of my eyes, all wild and bright hope, and you started to count down.

"Three." Inhale.

"Two." Hold it.

"One." Eyesshutandblowallthebreathoutandkeepblowinguntilyourlungsache.

Open eyes.

The seeds were parachutes of promise that teetered in the air.

The dandelion was bald.

We both smiled as we stared at it.

* * *

August, I don't quite remember when I locked you out of my life or forgot about our promises. As every memory slams into me, I taste the bitterness of regret. I walk into your home and go up the stairs. Your bedroom door is locked now, but that doesn't keep me out.

You don't go to school. You don't even leave your room. You are lying on your floor amid the wreckage that you created and you stare at the ceiling. I lie down beside you and my breath catches when I see it. There is a canvas pinned to your ceiling.

You painted me as if I was the sky, and my freckles the constellations. You painted me wild and wondrous. You painted me and I want to stand up and feel every brushstroke. When I stand, I see in faint white letters in the corner a date.

The date you must've painted this. The date was last week.

The thought tickles something in my chest, a memory, a feeling, but I can't place it.

I had still been alive. You painted me in stars as if I could be beautiful enough to be among them.

12

Magic,

In August's room, I see a little note in gold ink in my handwriting. I could only see the very first line.

Once upon a time . . .

I should've told August the truth about fairy tales and happy endings.

But when I see that note, I remember that I once believed in magic.

And it lived in gold ink.

There was a gold felt pen in Sheldon's corner store in the center of town. It was a tiny display of bright metallic pens that you could try on black paper. I would go there after school every day just to hold the pen in my hand. There was a feel to how it brushed the page, like an artful stroke. Like a soft kiss. The contrast of the gold shimmery ink and the stark black looked like magic.

I wanted to wield your power.

I wanted my stories and words to soak into that shimmering ink and grow wings.

The pen was such a simple thing. It sat in a plastic display and the black paper had expletives and initials and inappropriate doodles. Other town kids came here to mess with the new rack of pens, but none of them knew how to wield the magic in them. Not like me.

It cost only $3.79. But I didn't have $3.79.

I just had two hands, two eyes, and one heart.

I walked out of the store with the pen hiding in my pocket.

I stole the pen.

It was wrong. I knew that. I could feel the trespass like an itch in my hand and when I was older, I left the money on the counter for Sheldon to find. He never knew I stole the pen, but that didn't matter. I knew.

I still used it.

I used it to unbreak my heart on sad nights and write new worlds with August.

Magic pinched between fingertips.

Until the ink faded and dried up, it let me hold your power, your freedom, in my hands.

13

Momma,

I needed that magic for what came later that year. I even had the pen in my back pocket when it happened. Father's anger seeped into the floorboards and doorframes. We could feel it everywhere, lurking and hungry.

When I was eleven, there was a day he had a late-night shift and wouldn't be home until after midnight. When I came through the door, I saw the grocery bags. I could smell the sweetness in the air.

"Momma, what's—"

You appeared in the kitchen doorway, your smile bright. There was flour on your shirt. "You got straight As this quarter, little dove. We need to celebrate." Your makeup covered old bruises, but your eyes were soft and warm and gooey.

Even though Father wasn't home, I walked in slowly, listening to the creaking floorboards, making sure not to let the surge of giddy excitement bubble up and make a mess. You sensed my apprehension, and just as I was about to say my protest, a handful of flour puffed against my chest. I looked down, white on my T-shirt. I looked up, innocent face and a waving powdery hand.

The burst of laughter was so shocking that I clapped a hand over my mouth the second it was out. I lunged for you.

The war of sugar and flour was on. We were childish and ridiculous and for that hour, you smelled of burnt sugar and everything I had missed about you. Our kitchen turned into a flour and frosting war zone and we were ruthless opponents. In lieu of helmets, you had a strainer on your head and I had a bowl. I stood on one side of the kitchen island as you kneeled on the other.

"One, two, three . . ."

"Go!" I said, jumping out from behind my side of the island and taking a big handful of flour to throw at you. You made a horrified expression as if I had caught you completely off-guard.

You threw a candy corn at me. "I am going to get you!" you said in an over-the-top troll voice, and you stood up, arms outstretched, and started chasing me. The floor was covered in flour and my sides hurt from all the giggling.

We didn't hear the car. Or the door opening. Father wasn't supposed to be home for hours. We were supposed to be the only two people who ruled over our little home at the end of Sunset Street. I was laughing when I felt you freeze.

That's when I heard it. It sounded like a growl but came out of a man. It scared me and I looked to the doorway.

"What's this?"

"Abel, I didn't know you were coming home early tonight. I was going to have everything cleaned up before you got home." Your eyes looked over the kitchen, wincing at the mess.

"I see I have some very naughty girls." Father wasn't yelling. He was leaning against the doorframe. "What should I do with you now?"

He didn't look scary. But when I looked at him, I was afraid. I had never been afraid in my own house before he lived with us. I had liked the dark, I had played in the basement, I had stopped using a night-light. I was brave. That's what you said, but I didn't feel brave when I looked at Father. I felt small.

"I'm sorry, Abel. I'll start cleaning up now." You stood up and whispered "Go to your room" under your breath to me. You held my arm and angled me to step behind you toward the door. I wouldn't budge. I wanted to stay as close to you as I could. This was our fault. Our mess. I didn't want you to be alone.

You shot a frantic look at me before returning your gaze to Father. "Are you hungry?"

He detached himself from the doorframe and took slow steps toward us until his face was an inch from yours. "This is not how I like my woman to behave, Regina." He raised his hand to your cheek and stroked it. "You know that."

Father looked away from you for a second and his gaze settled on me. He looked like a giant. "Ellie, do you know what we do with girls who don't listen?" Then he smiled at me.

I was about to muster an answer when his arm cocked back and crunched against your face. I screamed as you fell to your knees, nose bleeding. I kneeled down and wrapped my arms around you.

"Momma!" You tried to push me away, but I held on as tight as I could. A rough hand yanked me off you and I turned, swinging my arms trying to hit the giant back. "I hate you!" I screamed. "I hate you!" In one swift motion, he reached for his pants' belt buckle and pulled it from his belt loops.

"No. Abel, no!" I heard you scrambling to your feet behind me, but it was too late.

The belt hit me. And then again. I screamed. My knees buckled.

You lunged over me and held me under you, your back exposed to him.

I shook within your arms. I cried with each slap. They kept coming, steady and certain, and with each blow, you squeezed me tighter.

Then suddenly, the belt stopped.

Father grunted. He put his belt back in place, knelt beside our shaking bodies, and whispered, "Now clean up this mess." He walked out of the room, the flour sticking to the soles of his boots.

You sat up, heaving in breaths. You rubbed my back gently and whispered, "Are you okay, my little bird?"

I blinked at you. You'd never called me that before, but I nodded anyway. "I'm fine, Momma. But what about you—" I reached up to check your back, but you shrugged me away.

You nodded quickly. "I'm fine, dove. Go upstairs to your room. I am just going to clean up."

I did. I fell asleep before you had come up, but I heard something in the middle of the night that woke me up. It was a soft and broken sound. I stood up and padded to the hallway and creaked open the bathroom door. The TV was still on downstairs. There you were. Shirt off and staring in the mirror. Your back was awful—bloody, bruised. You were crying there in the bathroom. I wanted to go in and ask you if you needed a hug, but somehow I knew . . . I wasn't supposed to see.

I left you there with your tears.

14

Magic,

    I believed in you, but sometimes your ink was dry when I needed you most.

15

Momma,

I walk back home in the dark and hear the rumbling of a thunderstorm in the distance. I am not afraid of it. I stand at the bottom of the steps to our home. Our porch greets me, solid and tired. I put my hand on the railing. The memories are coming easier now. They know I will keep my eyes open. They know I won't look away.

* * *

I remember another day on this porch. You were sitting watching the sky and I sat on the steps on the other side of the screen door watching you. You had a cigarette in one hand and your head rested on the other. I hated the smell of the smoke. You had always smelled of honeysuckles from our adventures when I was little, and burnt sugar from your delicious southern baking.

But we didn't have adventures anymore, or sweets in the oven. The smell of Father invaded everything, until finally you started to smell the same. The screen was tattered at one edge and the mosquitos flew in along with the thick, humid air. Father wasn't home yet, but another storm was blowing in. One of rain and thunder and not rage and fists. And you sat there watching the sky get darker and pull closer. I leaned forward to get a better view of the black clouds and the step creaked.

You didn't turn your head. "Hey, my little dove." You took another drag from your cigarette. "Come sit by your momma."

I stepped down the creaking steps and opened the creaking door and sat down on the steps beside you. I breathed in the electricity in the air and tried to exhale all the smoke and himness stuck to your skin. "Shouldn't we go inside, Momma? The storm is coming."

"Oh, that little thing can't chase us inside, dove."

I looked out over the horizon past the rowhomes and trees. A spike of lightning. A gray-and-black sky swallowing up the blue. It looked like just the storm to chase me off the porch, but I sat there anyway.

I loved our porch, even if we only looked out over

cracked asphalt and boarded-up windows. It was a little space that was ours. We'd sit out there for hours when Father worked late. It was just outside the door, but we could breathe. We didn't feel trapped or suffocated; we drank in the air and tilted our heads back and drank up the sun too.

"We had a porch like this in Louisiana," you said, head tilted back, eyes closed.

"Did you like it in Louisiana?" You never talked much about your past, but I wanted to know.

You tucked your chin and slowly opened your eyes. "Our house was small, smaller than this one." That was hard to believe, because even though we had ample space (something I knew not everyone had), it always felt like the walls were closing in. "But it had a porch just like this one. We'd board it up when hurricanes were brewing. We'd sit in the dark as the wind rattled the shudders and the rain pounded the tin roof." And then you smiled and smooshed the edge of your cigarette into the side of the doorframe to snuff it out. It seemed strange to smile while recalling a natural disaster.

"But . . . did you like it?"

You turned your gaze to me. "I loved it."

You pulled up your knees under your chin. "On those days with hurricanes, when we were all huddled in the living room, we'd sing. We'd sing loud and then louder. We'd sing until the wind and rain no longer scared us, because when our voices seemed to win against the howling outside, we felt stronger than it."

I smiled at you, but as I did you blinked fast and looked away. The smile settled back into your usual set of lines, your usual far-off gaze that felt just out of my reach. I didn't want to say anything just in case your smile came back, just in case it was a fragile scared thing and I could coax it to return if I was quiet.

It was then that I tried to remember your singing and couldn't. A sliver of a song caught in the wind from the car's open window, a soft melodic hum as we held hands and walked down the street when I was little. But even those memories had been vague and no matter how hard I tried, I couldn't remember what your voice sounded like.

We sat on our porch silently until your summer-sweet voice shook. "I haven't felt strong in a very long time." You didn't look at me. You just reached your hand over and squeezed mine. Then you stood up and walked silently back into the house.

The house that never heard you sing.

16

House,

I stare up at you. You are scruffy paint, creaking steps, and broken glass. You tucked our tears and fears into your nooks and crannies. Our whispered prayers stained your floorboards. You never heard songs, but you heard my last breath.

Maybe you were never trying to trap us in.

Maybe you were trying to hold us together.

17

Father,

The house didn't need to hold us together before you came with your sad-puppy eyes and fists. Before you came with such pretty words and gentle embraces. You were the burn and the balm at the same time. You were Tabasco sauce and warm apple cider. Because just when we would scurry off into our silent rooms, you'd coax us out with your rumbling voice and tuck us into your arms as if you forgot that you hurt us with those same hands.

We lied to you too. With our smiles and apprehensive glances. But also with our little secrets. Momma begged you to let her have the job. I went with her to the Dixie and the manager said it would be $14.35 an hour. She asked to be paid in cash. When she got home she told you that the job paid eight dollars an hour. I almost corrected her, but the look she leveled on me—not in anger but a wordless plea—kept me quiet.

You didn't give her an answer. Then a few days later, an old minivan was parked outside in our driveway. It looked like our old one. It had the same mismatched doors. This was your answer. Your act of love and mercy. She could get the job.

That month, Momma stopped smoking.

18

Momma,

You are staring at the flowers in the middle of the dining table. Father left them there for you.

Father would always bring you roses or daisies or whatever was in the $4.99 flower bin at the supermarket after a rough night or a fight or a drunken beating. I always loved their colors and how delicate the petals looked in the sunlight. You would always smile. Always say thank you. Always fuss over taking care of them right away: looking for the chipped glass vase in the cabinet, cutting the ends of the stems at an angle, putting a little sugar in the water.

I think Father thought it was a cheap way to make you

smile, but he never noticed how you looked at the flowers when he looked away. You'd skin chicken and your eyes would scan the flowers, cut end to bloom and you'd furrow your brow and look out the window with sad eyes. That's how you look at them now.

One day when Father worked late, we played in the fields behind the school. Patches of wildflowers sprang up in the tall grass and I remember reaching down to pluck some.

"No!" you said, your voice was sharp and sudden and made my hand snatch back. You saw my expression and your face softened. "No, little dove. Don't pull the flowers."

"Why not?"

You were quiet for a moment and then motioned for me to sit beside you in the grass. "It—it is selfish to pluck something just because you want to keep it to yourself. The flowers die faster."

"But lots of people have flowers . . ."

I looked at the flowers. They swayed in the breeze and danced in the grasses, innocent and unaware.

"Just leave them there, dove. We can sit with them. We can love them even if we don't take them home."

And so we stretched back and lay there. Breathing in the warm air and the smell of wildflowers, eyes up to blue skies and wispy white clouds, holding each other's hands.

❋ ❋ ❋

You leave the flowers on the table.

19

Funeral Director,

Momma never answers when you call, but I hear your voice beep in on the answering machine every day.

You speak in a cadence and tone that sound too bright and breezy for a call about dead daughters. Momma is about to click delete on your message when your voice pitches up in a singsong melody. "A teacher from your daughter's school has sent lilies for her service. They are lovely and we just need to . . ." You never say my name. You speak as if my momma isn't replaying your message on the other end, shaking. You speak, unhearing, as Momma tears through the cabinets and finds the chipped glass vase and throws it against the wall.

You speak as Momma falls to her knees and grasps the glass in her hands just to let them bleed.

And when you say goodbye, Momma is crying.

I wonder if she is thinking about blue skies and wild-flowers.

I lie down beside her and stare at the cracked ceiling as she weeps.

20

Momma,

The memories slip and slide and I feel unsteady.

You and Father are at the dining table.

I sit where I usually do at the end of the table. Watching. Just watching.

Your face is still painted like a clown with too much color. You sit at the table and I can tell something is missing, though I'm not sure what it is. I study the makeup, the heavy mascara and eyeliner, the plumpness of your red lips, the way that your hair is curled perfectly to frame your face. Not a strand out of place.

So what is it? What is the "it" that is missing? You eat

your food quietly, one hand on the spoon, one in your lap. You look smaller somehow. You were always taller than me, but now it looks like the chair could swallow you up. You aren't slumped over or crying anymore. You are there like any other Thursday, eating your dinner and itching to leave.

That is when I see it: a tear in the vinyl plastic tablecloth covered with baskets of oranges by the hundreds, the one from the downtown Dollar City faded to a deteriorating yellow. I hated that tablecloth. It's old and ugly and I remember trying to count all the baskets at breakfast just so I didn't have to look up. But that rip . . . I've never seen it before. I stare at it. It's a small slit about an inch wide that cuts straight through a basket. It isn't far from where I used to sit, where I sit now; it's nearly at the halfway point between where you and I sat, so why didn't I see it?

I clench my eyes shut. Something used to be there; something covered it up. A plate? A glass. My eyes open wider, remembering.

No. A hand.

Your hand. It was always there, delicately placed on top of the cut, your fingers relaxed and slightly spread out, your arm extended just a little too much for comfort.

A hand. For me.

I was the one who was supposed to see it. The way your hand was like an offering, reaching. *I'm here,* your hand had said.

I stare at the spot now. The spot without your hand to

cover it. Hadn't I seen the way you snuck glances at me? I thought they were silent pleas to behave, to not say a word. I thought they were a silent chastisement. But they weren't, were they? Your eyes were pleading. Not for me to behave. Not for me to be quiet. But for me to see you reaching. Your eyes never lingered long. For fear that Father would catch you? Or because I never looked back?

I remember holding your hand as a child. Your hands had been so big and warm and soft. I remember knowing, right down to my bones, that your hands would keep me safe. I hadn't felt that way in a long time, but then again, I hadn't held your hand in a long time.

I remember that hand that had seemed so innocently placed; I remember catching glimpses and seeing how there were tiny spiderwebs of lines, wrinkles, and pink knuckles; pale skin, calluses, and a cut; ragged cuticles, bit fingernails, and chipping nail polishes. You didn't care what your hands looked like. You didn't cover them up because the bruises weren't there. But I saw the ruined part of you that told tales in something as inconsequential as the skin on your bare hands. And those real, naked, ruined hands had been there reaching for me.

And I never reached back.

Now, you sit unreaching because you think there isn't anything to reach for. I stare at you and I see it. That "it" that is missing. Your eyes are counting the baskets, far-off and resigned. Nothing glimmers or shines in your eyes and

I feel like it is a punch to my gut that I never saw it before. You had plans, didn't you? I can see it . . . the way your eyes had always been here, but not really. Something was ticking and gears were turning, and I just didn't see.

Now you don't have any plans. Nothing is clicking, turning, or cranking. Your eyes are dead.

Just like mine.

But you aren't dead.

Not yet.

And I wish your hand was propped up over that broken basket . . .

And I wish, and wish, and wish that your eyes still shone, because they were beautiful and secret.

I miss your beautiful secret eyes.

21

Momma,

Father is snoring in your bedroom. You had stayed quiet all evening, but once he fell asleep, you went into my room. You must've scoured through it while I was at August's house. You found my stash of Ms. Hooper's papers beneath a stack of my books and they are in a neat pile on the floor.

You take in a deep breath and walk toward my bed. You kneel next to my mattress as if in prayer, which strikes me as strange because you haven't prayed in a long time. I guess pain pushes us back to our knees sometimes. Pushes us until the only place we can set our sights is up; otherwise, we break.

You put your fingers under my mattress and then lift it. I frown. It feels like an invasion. I want to slap your bandaged hand away. I run forward, but then I see the hole in the box spring. A neat square where a box is hiding.

You pull it out and open it. I kneel beside you, watching how your shoulders shake.

I gasp in a breath. Money. Pamphlets. A letter. And on top of it all . . .

I see *them*.

They have discolored with age. There are rips around the edges, but I recognize them.

My shoulders tremble right next to yours, because I remember and I am ashamed that I ever forgot.

* * *

It was a Monday. I was twelve. August wasn't able to come by to wrestle in the woods that day because I was sick. I didn't like being sick, not just because I didn't like the way my head ached and my nose was snotty and everything felt heavy, but also because it meant I couldn't go to school. You stayed home to take care of me.

"I'm old enough to stay home alone, Momma."

"I know, dove. You are a young lady now, but it would make me feel better to make sure everything is all right. Is that okay?"

I shrugged. "Sure."

You smiled and put the thermometer in my mouth.

"I am glad not to go to work anyway. My feet are getting tired," you said, pulling out the thermometer. Then as if forgetting, you jerked your face to me and said, "Just don't . . . Just don't tell your father that."

I blinked, not seeing how that would be something that would matter, but nodded. You relaxed and looked at the thermometer reading. "Oh, my little bird, you have a fever." You pressed your lips to my forehead. "I hope you feel better. You have to rest today, but is there something you want to do? Something special? Something that would make you feel better?"

The thought was unprovoked, but hit me all the same. I thought of sunlight and windshields and feet propped up on dashboards. I thought of cheering every time we saw a new town's welcome sign. I thought of driving and having no destination and the freedom of just laughing and singing while strapped into seat belts. We were free and safe. I looked at you and you looked back, expectant and smiling. "I would like to go for a drive . . . like we used to."

Your smile faltered, even though you tried to keep it in place. You sighed and I saw how your shoulders fell. The excuse was coming. I looked away from you toward the window. You were about to say something and I cut you off as I mumbled, "Never mind."

"I—"

"Just let me rest, Momma, okay?"

I rolled away from you and buried my head in the pillow.

No drives, or rolled-down windows, or treasure hunts, or climbing, or wide-open spaces where there was just road and us. Only here. Beer cans overflowing the recycling bin, and the smell of too much dust and too little air—everything stagnant and stuck and unmoving and trapped. My mattress pitched up as I felt you stand up and leave the room.

Step. Step. Step.

Always walking away. I hugged the pillow tighter, actually grateful that everything felt so heavy because then I felt like I could become one with the mattress and the pillow, and turn invisible. I wanted to cry, but I thought of Father's belt. He wasn't here . . . but what if he found out?

I almost didn't hear your steps as you came back into my room; I was so focused on not crying. "All right, my dove! Outta bed!"

I looked up and saw you smiling with a small basket in your hand.

"What do you mean?" I stared at you, confused.

"Well, I think that my little bird asked for a drive, so we better get going."

I sat up, curious but hesitant. "What's in the basket?"

"Food . . ." You grinned. "And a treasure map."

The smile was involuntary, uncontrolled. I couldn't hold it back even if I'd wanted to, and I didn't want to. Despite the headache, I swung my legs out of bed and raced to the car. "I am going to beat you!"

You laughed behind me, chasing me, but keeping your pace just slow enough so that I could win. I knew you did, but it didn't make victory any less sweet. I opened up my car door and sat in the front seat. The sticky leather didn't feel uncomfortable like it usually did. I rolled down the window and clicked on my seat belt.

You scooted into your seat after putting the basket in the back seat. "So, where do you think the treasure map will take us?"

I looked up and down the street. Left was school, but beyond it was where Father worked, and that didn't feel like the right way to go to have an adventure. I pointed to the right. "That way!"

"That way it is, my little bird."

I smiled as you pulled out of the driveway. It was too hot. My nose was snotty and my throat hurt, but it was perfect. We turned right and drove straight out of town.

Blue Moon Mountain was almost an hour away. I squirmed in my seat until the car was parked in the lot and then we both flung off our seat belts as we stepped out. We used to come here all the time and set up a picnic off Sunrise Trail.

"That way!" I grabbed your hand and we skipped through trees and past boulders, going up, up, up until we saw it. The ruins of a stone building. We pretended that the stone structure was our castle and we were the queen and princess who ruled over all the acres that surrounded us. I was a warrior princess because I didn't want a prince to save me. I wanted to save us myself, and you let me. You would sit back and cry, "Oh no! Ellie! The dragon!"

I would raise my stick in the direction of the creature and stab. It all felt right and safe and possible then. Our picnic was water and peanut butter and jelly for you and Pedialyte and a peanut butter sandwich (no jelly) for me. You even cut the crust off. Father didn't let you do that, but you knew that was how I liked it best. I bit into my sandwich and I was happy. Just as happy as I was when I played with August or raised my hand at school, but for some reason, this was even better.

"We should do this all the time," I said. You paused before taking your next bite.

"We should. I miss our adventures."

I looked at you. "Why did we stop?"

Your eyes took on a distant look that I recognized and I wanted to take my words back to keep you with me.

"It doesn't matter," I said. "I am glad we could today." I smiled at you and was surprised at the way you looked at me. It was different from happy or sad or amused. You looked thankful.

"I am glad too." You set down your sandwich, reached into the basket, and pulled out two sheets of paper.

"Are we going to do homework?" I didn't mind, because I liked homework.

"No, I wanted to show you something." You pulled the page out and started folding it, one fold, then another, then another. It wasn't a paper airplane. Watching what you did, I tried to unlock the mystery.

"Do you know why I call you 'little bird'?" you asked.

You called me that for a long time. I remember thinking it was weird in the beginning. Who calls their daughter "little bird"? Then after a time I got used to it.

I shook my head and you continued folding.

"Birds can look like such small and delicate things. But as tiny as they are, they were born to fly." You finally stopped folding and put the little paper creature in your palm for me to see. It was white and delicate. Crisp lines created the bird's head and beak and the sleek folds of its wings.

I marveled at it. I snatched it away and cupped it in my hands. "It's beautiful! I love it!"

You smiled and started folding the other piece of paper. "You will fly away, my little bird." I heard a hitch in your voice as you continued folding. "You will fly high and so far away."

I looked at your hands and the slight way they shook as they folded, and folded, almost with urgency. "What is that one for?" I asked.

You finished and held the bird in the palm of your hand, bringing it toward me so that our palms were balancing the white birds side by side.

Your words were so soft. "So will I."

There was hope there. Real hope. The kind that was overflowing with truth and urgency, intention and plans.

We drove home late. You kept glancing at your clock and swallowing hard. I played with the pair of white birds in the car as I watched the sun turn orange and dip toward the mountains on the horizon in the rearview mirror.

I felt the squeeze in my chest as we got home. I didn't want to go home and unlock my seat belt and walk into the house, but as we drove up the gravel pavement, I knew I had to. With a sigh, I got out of the car. You took my arm and hurried me inside.

"Go wash your hands and face and get into bed."

"But why?"

"Just do it!" Your words were harsh and I could tell you regretted it by the shape of your eyes, but you didn't say sorry. I put our birds on the coffee table and bolted out of the room.

I ran upstairs and everything was starting to feel too heavy again; our castle felt a million miles away. I scrubbed my face, but some dirt refused to come off my cheek. I left it there, dried off with the towel, and went to my room. I heard the growl of the engine just as I was closing my door. That familiar engine that pulled into the driveway behind your mismatched-door van and blocked it in.

It took a while before I heard the squeal of the front door open. "Regina. Where did you go today?" The rumble of his voice, the calm before the storm, was a sound I knew by then. It was deceitfully soft, treacherously soothing. It could almost lull you to sleep if you weren't careful.

I heard your hesitant footsteps leave the kitchen and go to the door. "What—what do you mean?"

"What do I mean?" I heard Father's slow steps. "I mean, you left," he said. "And I want to know where you went."

A pause. I hugged my pillow tight. Maybe you would tell on me? Tell Father that I wanted to go to the mountains? Maybe he would punish me.

"I had to go to the store . . . to get Ellie medicine."

"Oh, is that right?"

The crack of palm to face was a loud one, and I knew the sound too well. I buried my head in the pillow. "Then why are there eighty-seven miles more on the odometer than there were this morning?"

Another slap. "Oh, Regina. Why do you make me hurt you? Why do you lie to me?"

I didn't hear you cry. And it wasn't until I heard the crash of glass that I bolted upright and stared at the locked door.

Should I go see?

I heard footsteps on the staircase, one pair, then the other. A shower turned on as the TV blared to life in your and Father's room.

The next day, I saw that there was no glass top on the coffee table, just the legs were left. That had been the crashing sound last night. You were already in the kitchen.

"Are you okay, Momma?" I asked. You smiled and I saw there was a cut on your lip that was masked by red lipstick.

"Of course, my little bird. Of course."

Father came down and sat at the table. I ate my cereal quietly, counting how many oranges were in each basket. It wasn't until I was grabbing my backpack and leaving the kitchen that I saw what was in the trash. A pile of glass and two white paper birds. I didn't reach in to get them.

We never drove out to the mountains again.

* * *

There they are in that box.

Two crumpled birds lying side by side on top of heaps of ones and twenties and fifties—money I know immediately that you must have been stashing away for a long time. You reach into the box and hold the origami birds, tracing the edges even though they are worn and might break. You take them in your ruined hands and press them to your heart. You start to speak, shaking your head from side to side with each word, and your chest creaks. I'm afraid your ribs may break.

Your voice is as fragile as the tattered paper birds. "I never meant for us to stay in this cage, my little dove. I always thought that we'd leave it. Together." You grit your teeth. "I just thought—I had time."

You open a bright blue-and-orange card and stare at its sparse prose as if it is an incantation. I peer over your shoulder and see it is a graduation card. Addressed to me. You had bought this before I died. I skipped over the little poem centered on the card—I never read those impersonal words—and went straight to your handwriting in gold Sharpie. You knew how I loved that gold ink. *We fly today, my dove! We are free.*

You tear it in two.

I stare. I stare even as it no longer sits in your hands. We were going to leave. Together. We were going to take this money and your minivan and we were going to leave Father and this damn house and this too-small life behind after I graduated. You had planned that all along.

And it is then that I want to disappear. I don't want more answers! I don't want to see any more because this hurts too much to hold. My hands are bleeding from its edges. My heart is splintering into pieces and I won't ever find them all.

You pick up a letter in the little box and unfold it. As I look over your shoulder, I see it isn't a letter at all. It is sheet music, and fluttering up and down the bars are notes, and crammed into the space between are lyrics. My name is in curling script across the top.

Your voice is a shiver in the dark. "I wanted to sing for you." You wipe your nose on your sleeve and give a half-hearted laugh. "You and your loud, blaring music. You'd probably hate all my songs." You fold the sheet music back into its neat little square. "But . . . they were still all for you."

I think of the hurricanes that couldn't steal your voice. I think of our home that never heard your songs. I think of how even the delicate notes of your humming were stolen by open windows. You said you used to sing because it made you feel strong and then in the quiet, in secret, you wrote your songs for me.

Your finger grazes the edges of one of the birds. "I was never brave enough to do so many things." You are trembling and I can't do anything about it. You are trembling and I just imagine all the nights I went to sleep thinking I was entirely alone and yet I had someone writing me songs that one day she would sing to me, one day when we were free.

I want to hear all your songs.

We sit like that for a long time. Tears and tattered edges.

You hadn't been weak all these years, even though I thought you were. You had been planning and that was what those beautiful secret eyes were all about. A box hidden in your daughter's mattress, stuffed with money and a pamphlet for trailers in Tennessee because you knew I loved the mountains, and two little birds that were made on a sunny day when the world was bright and full of possibility, and songs to make us strong for the journey as we kept our promises that we would fly away. But I left you.

I left you because I had forgotten. But you never did. You kept a treasure chest of hope by me so that I would be safe. You kept my door locked, your head down, your face painted, and your whimpers low because you were waiting for the moment . . . the right time.

The tears build in my eyes as I reach for you.

For our birds.

For the hand that reached over cut tablecloths.

And when my fingers slip through yours, earthquakes of pain and sorrow erupt inside of me. I shake in the dark so far away from you, yet I'm right here with the house as our only witness.

"I am sorry too, Momma. I am so sorry."

We are daughters of regret and shame and secrets, and we cry together until the clock chimes six a.m.

22

August,

I leave Momma's side and return to yours. The sky has started to bleed out its colors into the night. You are staggering with a beer in your hand. It pains me to see you so unsteady. I remember when we ran these same streets as children, every step purposeful and sure. We would always run to our sanctuary or to our bridge that went high over the river.

That is where you are walking now. I move in lockstep with you, wishing I were solid so I could grasp your hand and hold it in mine. But I can't, so I settle for staying close by your side. Minutes pass in solemn silence and then we step over the boundary between the Real world and the one we created together.

* * *

"Hurry up!" I yelled over my scrawny twelve-year-old shoulder. You were a few yards behind and I grinned like a wild woman at you. "Slowpoke! I win!" I drew out the *I* so that it would last. I drew it out until I crossed the threshold of the barn bridge and halted, my belly heaving in huge breaths. Sweaty and reddening, you slowed down to a walk before getting to me.

"You are a cheetah."

"And you're a . . . what? A sloth?"

You glared at me with your customary I-am-pretending-to-be-offended glare. I smiled back with my I-know-I-whipped-your-butt smile.

It took you longer to recover your breath.

Mondays. I loved Mondays. Father worked late, which meant I could pretend with you longer. I could run and be wild and free. We walked over to the barn bridge window and peered over the edge. "Ever think about jumping?" I asked.

You reeled. "From up here? Don't be ridiculous! See those rocks? That current? You jump from here and you're practically asking to kick the bucket."

"I guess I am just too reckless," I said, turning away from the window and toward the wood planks.

"Uh, yeah," you said as we both pressed our backs to the barn wall and slid to the ground.

"August?" I asked.

"Uh-huh?"

"We are . . . good . . . friends, right?" I asked, hesitation in my voice. I didn't want to go home, but I had to soon. I didn't like leaving you in the woods alone.

"The best," you said, and that made me grin.

"The best," I repeated under my breath.

"Yeah." You shifted and pointed to a wooden beam. "See, I'll show you." You took your Swiss Army knife out of your pocket—the one you were grounded for having a month ago—and started carving into the wood. *A&E BFFS*.

"I don't know. It doesn't feel very official."

You blinked at me and then shifted onto one scraped knee. You winced a little before smiling. "Ellie Walker, I, August Matthews, ask for your hand in holy best friendship."

I laughed and lightly punched you on the shoulder. "I accept. Gotta settle down some time or another."

You fake-glared again with your saucer eyes. "Settle? Excuse me, I am top-grade material. You should be so lucky. I think I deserve a better acceptance speech than that."

"Okay." I got on my knee. "My dear August Matthews, despite your sloth-like running skills that could never rescue me from a burning building, I accept your offer of holy best friendship because despite everything, you are, in fact, my best friend."

"I do," you proclaimed, chest puffed out.

"I do," I said reverently.

I leaned on a beam while you wrote *Till death do us part* underneath our names. I smiled as you carved the wood. With the last letter, you suddenly swiveled back toward me, looking mischievous. "Now, I can kiss the bride—I mean friend."

And you quickly leaned forward and did.

It felt funny to feel lips on mine. I hadn't thought about it before. Lips were for smiling and talking and making faces . . . but for kissing?

You leaned away, redder than when you were running, and jumped to your feet. "Race you to the houses?"

I cocked my head up at you. I wanted to ask about the kiss. Also, I wanted to ask how you knew I had to go home. And why you weren't making me feel bad about it. I didn't. "Of course." I started to get to my feet, but you were off.

"Cheater!" I chased after you and I loved how my heartbeat tripped over my breath as we ran away from our wonderland. We laughed with every step.

* * *

There is no smile on your face as you take another swig of beer and sit with your back against the faded barn wall. I stare at you. What are you doing, August? Graduation is soon and you are here drinking? I want to slap you.

There is a party tonight.

That's right, a senior party.

That's where you should be. Getting ready. Making wild memories with all the friends that think you are fifty shades of awesome, not here alone.

"Get your ass up, Matthews!" I yell at you, but you can't hear me.

You do get up to your feet and toss your beer bottle against the barn bridge wall. It shatters.

"You have to stop breaking stuff," I say to you, but then I am glad you can't hear me, because I am no one to make such a request.

I break too much.

I remember when everything began to change between us. I remember when the metaphorical wood branded with our BFF promise began to splinter.

* * *

Father stopped working late on Mondays and so our afternoons playing in our little grove came to an end. Our last Monday together was a hot June afternoon. It was the day before your birthday. We were leaning against our BFF board in the barn bridge and sort of leaning on each other as if the whole wall behind us wasn't quite enough. We each needed the other.

"Are you coming to my birthday party tomorrow?"

"You're having a birthday party on a Tuesday?"

"Yeah, why not? School is out."

I bit the inside of my lip. "What time?" If it was during the day, then maybe I could stop by . . . maybe I could have your mom pick me up?

"Seven p.m." You beamed. "Water fight. So don't wear a white T-shirt, 'kay, Boney?"

Usually, I laughed when you said things like that, or called me "Boney," but I didn't this time. Your smile faltered. "I—I was just joking. I didn't mean . . ."

"Oh no, it isn't that. I just . . . don't know if I can go."

"Why not?"

"I'm, uh, busy."

"Bull crap," you said matter-of-factly.

"What? I am."

"Ellie Walker, you are never busy. You are just home."

I stiffened. I didn't know what to say. I could lie, but then . . . would you know?

"I—I don't know if I can get a ride."

"Oh, that's no big deal. My mom can pick you up," you said, picking at the leaves stuffed in your laces.

"August, I just can't go, okay?"

Standing up, I turned back to you. "I can't come tomorrow. But, I'll get you something. I promise."

"I don't need a present, Ellie. I just wanted you to come." You shifted, straightening your legs as if you could actually block my path. I stepped over your outstretched legs.

I couldn't say that I wanted to go, because then you would press harder to convince me. You would get your mom to call my momma and then she would try to figure it out and I knew that while I was off somewhere pelting school kids with a water gun, Father would be home pelting her with fists. I couldn't do that to her.

"I can't," I said harshly.

You stared at me—your eyes somewhere past my head staring, glaring. "Fine."

I ran off.

Tuesday night I tossed and turned. Who would be there? What were they doing? Who won? Who sat next to you when you blew out the candles? I was jealous. I didn't remember the last party I had gone to and I wish I could've gone to yours.

The next Monday, I started lacing up my shoes at 3:47 p.m. I know because I had looked at the big clock in the kitchen and I was going to be late to meet you by the creek if I didn't run. FAST.

I stiffened when I heard it. A motor roaring down the street.

Please don't be him.

But it was him. He was home early. Hours early.

I stood up straight, cringing as I heard his boots on the porch steps, and then the door creaked open and he filled it. He stopped when he saw me staring. I thought, *This is the ogre who guards the bridge so that no one can ever leave.*

I knew then that I wouldn't see you that day.

I knew then that something was about to change.

23

Father,

That day, you looked down at me. You had been drinking. I could smell it on you. You blinked and narrowed your eyes at me.

"Hi, Father," I said quietly.

You rubbed your jaw and gave me a curt nod.

Your eyes didn't leave mine as you pulled off your shirt and went to sit in the living room.

I shifted my gaze away and looked at the door. The freedom just beyond it.

"Going somewhere, Ellie?" The rumble, the warning.

"No," I said quickly, looking back at you.

You were bare-chested. You took in a deep breath and then pulled a lighter out of your pocket. I hated that lighter.

While I stood there, between you and the door, I remembered that the first time I had seen your lighter was right after Momma started working, a couple of years before.

She had worked late and dinner hadn't been ready. You sat at the dining room table. Momma walked in, frazzled and already apologetic. There was a can of gasoline on the floor and she went quiet at the sight of it.

"I wondered if you'd come back, Regina."

That's when you pulled out your lighter. It was silver.

Click, open. Click, shut.

"I was thinking, well . . . if my woman isn't coming back, then maybe we should just burn the whole house down. You know, purge myself of the memories."

That's when Momma noticed me.

"Abel." Momma's voice was shaky. "Let's talk. Let Ellie go upstairs and let's talk."

"Oh." Click, open. Click, shut. "I belted her in. Didn't want her to miss it." Momma's eyes roamed over the leather belt and noticed how it looped around my waist and was buckled through the rungs of the wood chair's back like a seat belt pulled tight. I was trapped in the chair and eating ice cream. I hadn't really known to be scared when you did it. You'd said it was a game. You'd said it would be fun.

"There is no reason"—Momma approached slowly, arm

outstretched as if she were trying to pet a wild animal—"to involve Ellie in this, Abel. She's . . . She's just a child."

Click, open. Click, shut. "I don't like looking at her face."

Momma blinked at you. "What—why?"

"Because she looks so much like you."

* * *

I didn't remember the exact moment when I knew that the lighter was a threat, because on that day when I'd first seen the lighter, I had just been so happy to have peppermint ice cream. But somewhere between that day and the day I stood near the front door and you sat in the living room bare-chested, blocking my path to August, to freedom, I knew that your clicking lighter was a promise of pain.

I wasn't facing you when you said, "You look so much like your mother."

I swallowed. Frozen in place. That's what you had said that day. I knew it was a threat, and I didn't want to burn.

"She's taller than me," I said quickly. I needed something, anything to cast us as different. I looked for more things to say, but you said, "Come here," and it silenced me.

"Yeah, you look different. Your nose is mine, you're skinny like me, your face is just a bit wider. I am mixed up in there too. But you look like your mother."

I was waiting for a belt. For the gas can. For a slap. I clenched my fists.

But instead you sighed and said, "Your mother was beautiful."

I was so startled that I gasped. You laughed a little. "It's true. She was singing at this open mic spot back in New Orleans and her voice . . . mmmm, her voice just felt like velvet. I could feel it when I heard her. But then I looked up and I saw this gorgeous, wild-looking woman. A wild mare."

Your eyes were far-off, recalling. "I knew then that I had to have her. After her song, I went up to her and she smiled at me and I stayed in town and before long, she was mine." You smiled then, as if you were tasting chocolate.

I felt uncomfortable even though I liked imagining my momma as wild, as free, as someone who could hypnotize people with her voice. Like she was magic. I tried to remember a time when I had heard Momma sing, and beyond the hum of lullabies from long, long ago, I couldn't.

"But then your momma got a little restless. She wouldn't listen."

Lighter. Click, open. Click, shut. "She wanted to leave." The far-off-ness of your eyes came back and settled on mine, alert even in their whiskey haze. "And so I had to break her in and bridle her. I had to make her listen. Your woman should listen to you. And she just wouldn't. Then one day, she was gone."

You sat up, leaned forward, eyes dark. "She left me . . ." you said, pointing at yourself, "because of you." Your finger then turned on me and even though there was distance between us, I felt like you had stabbed me.

"You have some of me in you, sure," you said, leaning back in the seat.

Click, open. Click, shut. Jaw clenched, and unclenched. "But I see it in your eyes. That need to go, to get away, that restlessness . . ." He says that last word and he rolls his shoulders as if he is shrugging off revulsion. ". . . is from your momma."

I felt like I was going to cry. To say I'm sorry. I felt like I was going to bolt for the door and never come back. But you had found Momma, and you would find me too.

Your voice was as soft as a lullaby as you said, "And you will never leave me like she did."

24

August,

And I never did.

That's what I think as I look at you in the barn bridge.

The same day that Father told me how I would never leave him, you came to my house for the first time. I was upstairs.

I didn't go downstairs, but I did peer down through the banister. No one, NO ONE, ever came knocking at our house. The lonely house four down from the corner. But that night at 7:09, someone did.

And that someone was you.

Your second round of door taps was interrupted by Momma flinging the door open to poke her head out.

"Is Ellie home? I was supposed to meet her—" you said.

"Oh, young man, Ellie won't be able to go out and meet you on Mondays anymore."

There was a silence and then your voices were hushed whispers. After a moment, Momma closed the door and caught me watching.

She gave me an apologetic look.

I was slammed with anger, with shame, with one million bits of frustration.

She stayed with *him*. She brought him into our lives. She had been too wild and restless. She had a voice like velvet.

Her.

Her.

Her.

And that is when instead of nodding or trying for a smile, I glared at her and mouthed *I HATE YOU* through the banister bars. I was in prison and she'd put me there.

It didn't matter that we were warriors in our wonderland, August. In the Real world, we were just kids stuck on the opposite sides of my house's old oak door.

* * *

School let out for the summer shortly after that day and I barely saw you for weeks. I had felt guilty all summer long.

I had felt like I had abandoned you, betrayed you. I thought it would be different when I went back to school.

But it only got worse. It wasn't all at once—the break. It was slow. Bit by bit.

I remember you yelling "Hey, Boney!" at me at school one day in early autumn. It had recently become your nickname for me. I didn't mind it. It was pretty accurate. I wasn't like other girls in our grade. I didn't have boobs or hips. I hadn't even gotten my period yet. My bones jutted out from my shoulders and my hips, and my legs were like sticks that I shoved into my pants and shoes. It wasn't because I didn't eat. It was my body. I was just . . . that way. You knew that and you knew that it didn't bother me when you called me "Boney." It sounded like a term of endearment from you.

But when Britney sneered it at me in Anatomy class, it wasn't endearing at all.

"Hey, look! This is what Ellie looks like!" she said, laughing as she pointed at the skeleton named Carl who was hung up at the front of the classroom with a top hat and bow tie. Other girls looked between the skeleton and me and started laughing. "Oh my gosh! It does!"

"Shut up, Brit," I said under my breath.

It was seventh grade, a time when everything felt awkward and I was somehow a loser for not emerging from summer a sort of slutty Barbie doll. I still wore jeans that were ripped at the knee, a T-shirt, and hand-me-down sneakers. I had already found my white Converse shoes and had started writing on them, but they were under my bed, too big for me.

I had grown—just not in the boobs-and-hips depart-ment. I was tall. Really tall. Taller than all the girls in my class, and I was afraid that my clothes, being a size too small, would show things I didn't want seen. So during the first couple weeks of school, I wore Momma's shirts from the grocery store and an AREN'T MOMS GREAT? T-shirt that were both way too big on me. I missed my old band tees, but I couldn't fit in them anymore, and even though other girls showed off the tops of their arms and their midriffs, I wouldn't. Or couldn't.

I felt lackluster and all I wanted to be was invisible.

August, you were so bright and vibrant and colorful. Literally. You had started painting and your jeans would have splatters of yellows, reds, and greens. You were a bright spot in my gray and I loved it. Even your ink and charcoal drawings felt alive in a way that I didn't.

I wanted to live in your drawings. Your parents knew you loved art. They didn't know that you wanted to go to art school one day. They didn't know that you dreamed in color and brushstrokes. I did.

The girls kept laughing and then Britney said, "August is so right, your name should be 'Boney.'"

I turned my head and looked at you. Obviously, you'd fix this. You'd make it better. Your saucer eyes blinked back at me and you were stammering, "No, I—I—mean . . ."

But your eyes shifted to Britney and you didn't say another word.

See, even he won't defend you anymore. You are alone. You'll always be alone. The thoughts bit at my heels.

"Thanks," I muttered at you. I had been so happy to see you after not seeing you most of the summer, but maybe I was a joke to you.

You came to my locker after class. "Ellie, I'm sorry. I should've—"

"Save it, Matthews." I wouldn't look at you. A lot can change over a summer. In a day. In a blink. I wasn't going to grasp at something that was slipping away. "I don't need your help."

I had let bitterness settle into my bones. I had thought that the August who had once been my friend wouldn't just sit in his seat and stutter a response in the face of Britney's gorgeousness. He would have rescued me.

You didn't.

After, you kept going to my locker, kept trying to pass notes to me in class. You drew me pictures and I threw them away.

The world was starting to shift to gray and I didn't have any space for your brightness. I hadn't wanted to stay close to you as you dated and kissed pretty girls. I hadn't wanted to be close to you just so you could leave me behind.

That's what I thought, at least. So I pulled our tether until it snapped.

As your last, desperate act, you asked a friend of yours to talk to me on your behalf until finally I wrote a note back:

I want a divorce from our unholy best friendship.

I didn't talk to you for the rest of junior high.

* * *

Right now, I honestly can't remember talking to you since that moment.

Now you are at our beloved bridge and are almost drunk.

I think about how we kneeled on scraped knees and were bound in holy best friendship. I remember what your lips felt like. Another memory tickles at my mind, but I can't place it. Lips on mine. Lips that make me feel bright and whole and new.

I sigh and lean close to you. Too close. I bring my lips to yours. Just a whisper away. Just a touch too far.

While I'm there, you let out a breath that resembles a growl and a sigh. I think how the muscles of the throat can splice together sounds and make new ones that forge their own meaning. Breaths caught between one emotion and the next.

I stay close to you. I watch the way your slight muscles contract under your T-shirt. The way your breath is so close that if I were alive and in front of you, you could make my bangs fly. One thing is true—I feel awake, buzzing, tingling, and intoxicatingly alive.

I dare not reach out, dare not break the illusion that I am not a shadowless ghost and that I am in fact here with you and you aren't staring through me, but at me, with those intensely gray eyes—eyes like storms that could sweep me away in their torrent. You growl-sigh again and back up, pressing against the wall, sliding down to plop ungracefully on the ground. Nothing about you is ungraceful. Except this.

The anger is gone.

That's when I see it.

In your eyes, a desperate, sad, wild thing.

And it scares me.

Because I know what you want to do.

Because I had been there . . . and done it already.

You get up, walking quickly.

You wanted to lose yourself. Let go. My eyes scan our surroundings and I hold my breath. Everything suddenly seems too pointy and dangerous and I want to lock you in your room and keep you safe.

But I can't.

You pull out a little Ziploc bag of pills from your pocket. You are swaying on your feet. You go and get another beer and pop the pills in your mouth and down it with several huge gulps. The beer is dripping from your chin.

You stumble, tripping over broken branches and falling to your knees. You crawl a few paces and retch into the green, overgrown grass. The pills are out of you, I think, but you are still heaving in air and coughing out spit. You are something other and it makes you look ugly. I never thought that you could look ugly, but you do now.

You are laughing and clawing at the air as if you don't know whether the air around you is hilarious or terrifying. Maybe you didn't cough up all of the pills? I see the shift in your eyes . . . as if you are seeing something that is there, but it's not. Sitting up abruptly, you begin to shift back. All terror now.

And for just a moment, I think you look at me. Your eyes, like a feather, graze mine softly before you pause, brow narrowing, sweat dripping.

"August?" I reach out.

And you scream. At first I think it is because you see me, but your eyes are settled beyond me, afraid. You're on your feet, clawing at the air as if bats are attacking you. You're desperately trying to make them go away. "Get OFF me!" you scream. Whirling, you stumble and trip away. I can't catch you despite my outstretched arms.

Then you stop. You are staring at the gap in the wood, where the little window opening in the side of the bridge shows the beautiful river churning and racing below. "Ellie?" Your voice is hoarse, broken.

I blink, waiting for you to turn around.

"August?"

You don't turn around, but take a step closer to the side of the bridge.

"Ellie . . ." Your voice hitches. "Is that you?"

I look at the spot where you were just staring, staring as if I am actually there looking back at you, but I'm not. I'm five paces behind you with nothing for you to see.

You take another step.

"Ellie, don't!" It's like a wail and a command forged together. Another mingle of emotion and words that makes something entirely new. Falling to your knees, you're reaching, shaking. "Ellie! Please!"

Your body is shaking so hard, it looks like you have the power to make the bridge rumble. You stretch out your arms as if you truly hope you can grasp the nonexistent me you're seeing. "Please—" Your voice cracks again as if something inside you reaches out to steal your words back and drown them. "I can't catch you."

I stare at you. I didn't know a strong person could break. I thought you had to be born ruined or be chipped away slowly over time. I didn't know that just one thing— one loss—could shred a person to pieces. But here is the evidence.

Two days ago, there was a boy named August and his smile was bright and beautiful and he played guitar, and made geeky, intelligent jokes, and could laugh off jabs and make girls blush, and all he was armed with was his notebook. Two days later, after an announcement made in a classroom, days skipped from school, and a bottle of pills purchased, here you are now at this ledge.

"No!" Your scream bellows out and knocks me back. Trying to stand, you fall and desperately drag your feet, half-crawling, half-stumbling, to the bridge wall.

You stare into the water as if you have seen me jump in. The moon glints off the current, beautiful and deadly. "No, no, no, no, no," you cry, shaking your head from side to side, choking on tears. Starting to rip off your shirt, you step up onto the ledge. "I'll catch you . . . I promise . . . I'll get you."

You are going to jump in.

You are going to die.

I rush toward you, reaching. Emotions go to war but none can win. Anger, fear, sorrow, and desperation reload their ammunition and shoot, piercing one another so it's all a bloody mess inside of me. I know I will fall right through you. I know that you are only two steps from jumping.

I lunge forward, hoping and not hoping, wishing and not wishing, but all I know is that I must . . . I *must* . . . I MUST reach you.

I crash into you imagining that you are solid in my arms, corded muscle. I imagine the realness and physicality of you shocking me. But as I reach my arms around you, my arms close on nothing but air. You are still moving, still stepping up higher onto the ledge. So I move with you, ready to fall all over again, just so you aren't alone.

Without warning, you stop. One leg out the window

and one inside, both hands braced in the in-between. Your breath is gasps, a rising chest and shaking shoulders.

The determination melts from your shoulders. You become limp against me. You bump your head softly against the wood. "You aren't there," you say.

You vomit again and then collapse to your knees. Defeated.

"I'm sorry," I whisper, and I am ashamed because sorry will never mean enough. It can't whiteout pain or loss or bruises or sorrow. A Band-Aid for a wound that is too big, but I say it again: "I'm sorry." You pull out of the opening and lean against the bridge wall. Sliding down the wall, you fall to the ground.

"I just wish you were here," you say to the darkness, to the shadows and the bridge and the night. "I just wish you were here. With me."

I stare at you, watching as the far-off-ness settles into right-here-ness. You don't see me, but you're coming back, the drugs wearing away in your veins, reality falling back into place.

And even though you can't hear the hitch in my voice, I whisper back, "So do I."

* * *

I remember learning in psychology class about how people suppress traumatic memories to keep their minds safe, to black it all out so they can keep going, and I suddenly realize that my selective memory hadn't been a cruelty, but a mercy. All leading to this moment. Because I am triggered by August's almost-death into remembering my own. I feel it then, like the whole ocean surging to swallow me up. It is a sea of memories and it is finally ready to meet me at the shore.

the year of graduation

25

Depression,

I didn't know what you were when you came sneaking under my window. I had known sadness. I had known loneliness. I had known anger and resentment and shame and fleeting numbness. I had known all those things. They would come and go, settling into the air and around my fingertips and eyelashes. A scream, a bruise, a curse, a door slam might've triggered it, but then I would grit my teeth and narrow my eyes, and with time, I would scare it off. The feeling would slink away. In a few minutes. A few hours. A few days.

But one day, you came. Seven minutes before my alarm.

My eyes opened and I didn't move. I just looked out the window.

I had always loved that window. It faced east and every morning, no matter if I had to clamp a pillow over my ears all night, I would wake up to a sunrise. And that morning, it was beautiful. The blue stretched its arms and slivers of sunlight crept their fingers up the horizon, casting shades of pinks and oranges in all directions. I would have usually smiled at that sunrise, but that morning I just looked at it.

I looked and felt nothing.

I felt like I was nothing looking at nothing.

I didn't see the peeling white paint on the window pane, or the inky etch marks I had made on the sill, or the portrait of sun and sky beyond the glass.

I just saw a window.

I saw a place from where I could jump.

I didn't move when my alarm buzzed.

I just kept looking at the window and wondering how long it would take to hit the ground.

26

August,

I was about to cross the threshold of my next class when I pulled out my Chemistry seating assignment sheet and stumbled to a stop. I was going to be wedged between Henry Jordan and you. I looked up. I could see the back of his short buzz cut and your shaggy mane of brown hair. I was to be squished between this new boy at school (I knew everyone in our class except him) and my old best friend who I had divorced when we were twelve years old.

I was quite certain the gods (if there were any) were trying to punish me.

You looked back at the door and smiled. It was the kind of smile that should be illegal.

For the past few years, I studiously avoided you. I had ignored the murals you painted during the art exhibitions, ignored your notes in my locker, ignored your name whenever it came up in conversation. I had blocked you out. My life had been so much easier that way. Letting you in had been a foolish risk with Father always looking over my shoulder, ready to pounce. At least this way, I was safe.

That's what I had told myself. But then you smiled at me from our Chemistry desk and I could not ignore you. First, you would be one of my partners for the rest of the year. And second, in all of this time of blocking you out, you became someone new, someone . . . beautiful. I scolded myself at the thought. Your hair had grown out and curled away from your chin. You had stubble on your jaw. And your eyes, those gray eyes, somehow had gotten even bigger, as if the whole world could fit inside them.

Stop smiling at me! I didn't move from the doorway. I was an awkward roadblock and people were pushing past me. You stood up and gestured for me to take my seat. I looked away from you. Outside. To all of the non-smiling things.

"Ellie Walker!" you said to me, still smiling, when I finally reached our desk.

"August Matthews." I tilted my head in greeting. You were far too bright and colorful. You were far too much and I wanted to dim you down like an Instagram photo.

140

"And Henry Jordan, right?" I said to the boy with the buzz cut sitting on the other side of my chair.

He startled at the sound of his name and looked at me and waved nervously. I smiled at him, suddenly feeling a little warmer to him just because he looked as unsure and unsteady as I felt.

I shuffled between the seats and breathed in deeply. The heavy, oppressive feeling, the sadness that often chased me into rooms and out of them, hadn't lodged in my chest yet. I was grateful for that, at least.

"Wow, Henry. You got a smile out of the infamously non-smiling Ellie Walker." You said it and that made Henry smile at me. It was a kind, puppy-dog smile. I smiled at him again. I felt you watching us, I felt you roll your shoulders and tap your knuckles on the desk.

"So," you said a little too loudly, "senior year. What are your plans?" It is hard to make conversation when you don't want to, and it is even harder to make conversation with someone when you strategically cut them out of your life for years. The words seem forced and simple and ridiculous. *What do you care what my plans are?*

Henry answered first. "I am getting ready to apply to schools for pre-med."

"Oh," I said. "That's impressive."

Another puppy-dog smile in response. I suddenly wanted to pet his buzz cut.

"I am looking at schools for business." Your legs stretched out under the table. You were seventeen. Your voice was rougher than when we were kids and yet it was still so familiar, like the whisper of a memory. I blinked at you from under my veil of side bangs.

"Business," I repeated.

"Yeah, business," you said back. You looked confused and uncomfortable with the obvious disbelief in my voice.

I blinked again. "Not . . . art school?"

You shrugged.

I suddenly felt betrayed. It was irrational. It was dumb. But you had been the boy of brushstrokes and color, the artist who made drawings I wanted to live in. I sighed. I really didn't know you at all.

"Original," I said finally.

You fake-glared at me. It had been so long since I had seen that expression. I thought my heart would explode and be a catastrophic mess on the table between us.

"Ah, I see you are trying to mortally wound me, dear Ellie, by hurting my pride. But alas, you have already done that, yet here I am, still standing."

"Sitting."

"What?"

"You are sitting." I tried to push past the way you said "you have already done that," and so I decided to talk about my plans.

"I don't know what I am going to do yet, but . . ." I paused. I had never said it aloud. I had only written it in my diaries. But the year would be full of moments all about

142

looking forward and so that was what I was going to do. "I want to be a writer."

"A writer," you repeated back to me, but it didn't have the edge of disappointment that my voice had when I'd replied to your future plans.

Still, I wanted to shove it back into my head. I wanted to keep it hidden. Far away from judgmental eyes. But you didn't look like you were judging me. You looked like you were piecing a puzzle together.

"That's nice," said Henry. "Like a journalist?"

I shook my head and tapped my foot on the linoleum. I was wearing my inked-up shoes. There was barely any white space left on them. "No, like a novelist."

Henry was about to say something, but you interrupted him. "What do you want to write about?"

Write about what you know. I had read that in a book once and like a tidal wave, I was slammed with feeling lost and cold and uncertain.

"I want to write about broken things," I said softly.

Your gaze whipped to me, suddenly serious. Your eyebrows scrunched up together so high that I thought they looked like two caterpillars aiming to take flight right off your face.

Mr. Jameson walked in, ten thousand watts of scientific enthusiasm. He knocked into the skeleton and nearly walked straight into his desk.

We all turned our attention to the front of the room.

You chewed on your lip for a moment, then leaned closer and whispered, "I want to know about broken things, Ellie."

I didn't look back at you.

"My mad scientists! It is time to . . ." Mr. Jameson's voice bellowed throughout the classroom, nearly outdoing the ten thousand watts of Jameson-ness he walked in with. It was like he swept up all the air and there was only enough for him to speak.

I was grateful. I hadn't wanted to talk to you about broken things.

I didn't want to tell you that I was one of them.

27

August,

That first week back passed quickly, and suddenly it was time for Chem again. Thank god for block schedules so I didn't have to sit next to you every day.

I squeezed past your seat to get to mine. You didn't move, didn't even look up. Henry's seat was empty. I dropped my book and notebook on the desk and made a big show of arranging my space so I wouldn't have to look at you either. You felt too close. I felt like you already knew too much. I opened up the textbook and started reading intently. Well, fake reading. I could feel you shifting beside me, turning your head ever so slightly. I kept reading. Not really seeing the words as my eyes scanned and just blurred them all together.

"Ellie . . ." Your voice was tentative and quiet.

"Shhhh, I am reading."

"Ellie . . ."

I whipped my head to the side, annoyed. "What?"

Your eyes went wide and apologetic. You lifted your chin to the book. "Um, your book is upside down."

I blinked at you, then snuck a glance at the text. It was, in fact, upside down.

I closed the book and held it to my chest. "I was . . . trying something." What in the world was I talking about? Is this what happens when you do something ridiculous? You come up with even more absurd things to say? I wanted to smack my forehead with my textbook, but that also seemed, well, ridiculous.

"I am sure you were."

I looked at you.

You were smiling.

"Stop that."

"What?" You didn't stop.

"Smiling. You look ridiculous."

"Says the girl who reads books upside down."

"Listen, I—"

"You really should fix that habit because when you write your books it will be hard to write them that way."

I stilled; my body went rigid. Where was Henry? Where

was Mr. Jameson? Their cue to interrupt was sounding. Yet they'd missed it.

"*If* I ever become a writer . . ."

"You will be a great writer, Ellie." You said it in a rush. You said it like you'd been waiting to say it for hours.

I tapped my foot, drumming it to take out some of the nervous energy. "Why do you say that?"

You were quiet for a second and then with your eyes far away you said, "Because once upon a time, you dreamed up a world for us to live in behind an old subdivision in the woods. It was real. It was ours. And it was beautiful. You'll write like that. You'll make things real with your stories."

I felt my eyes go glassy, not because of the familiar ache in my chest that kept growing, but because it was like you had plucked out my future dream and said it aloud when I was too afraid to say it myself. You had thought a long time about what you were going to say. I could see that.

Henry sat in his seat next to me. The bell was about to ring and then I heard your voice go softer, go deeper, as if this was something you had waited even longer to say. "Besides, you know all about breaking things."

28

Depression,

You liked to tell me stories. Tragedies. The tragedy of me. I stood staring in mirrors wondering where the bits of me had been left behind. When I looked into my eyes, they didn't often seem like my own. You'd whisper the end to the story in my ear. A window. A rope. A cut. A pill. The method changed. But the ending was always the same: I would be gone.

Your stories scared me.

But I listened.

And they were a secret, because I was too afraid to say them aloud.

29

August,

The next day, you tugged on my sleeve when I was sitting down in Chemistry.

"What?" I practically barked at you.

"I'm sorry," you said, hands up in surrender. "I shouldn't have said what I said."

Instead of accepting your apology, I asked, "Why aren't you going to art school?" I still couldn't force the disappointment out of my voice. I tried, but I failed.

You swallowed hard. "I—I just couldn't ask my parents. I couldn't tell them that I wanted to be an artist."

I tensed. You *couldn't* tell them? I breathed through my nose and tried to keep the annoyance out of my voice.

"Why not?"

"I mean, my dad is this business exec and my mom was a lawyer before she had me and it just felt, I felt . . ."

I waited.

". . . that they couldn't accept it."

"Did you even ask?"

You raised your eyebrows as if the question never occurred to you. "No . . . They asked me what I wanted to do after high school and I was sitting there at the dining room table and I just felt so much pressure, you know? They let me do art, but I knew they thought I would give that up and grow up when I left for college. So when they asked, I just blurted out 'business school.'" You sighed. "You should have seen my dad's face, Ellie. He was so happy, so proud. I just . . . I don't want to take that away from them."

You were doing business because you felt you had to, as if you were cornered into it, as if you had no other choice. I knew what that felt like. I stopped going to the woods all those years ago with you because I felt I had no choice. But you did have choices, you were just afraid to make them.

"You shouldn't do things you don't want to just because you think that's what other people want," I said.

You ran your fingers through your hair. "I wish I could believe that."

"You should."

"And how would that story go? Son of business execu-tive and former lawyer goes to the big city to become an artist and instead camps out in a box with his crayons because lo and behold, the starving-artist stereotype is true."

I was annoyed. The August I knew, the August of light-ning bugs and vivid brushstrokes, wasn't this cynical people pleaser. He was a dreamer. He could paint magic doors to Anywhere.

"Once upon a time, there was a boy who could paint the world with his fingertips. He didn't know that with every brushstroke he made, people felt more real, or that with every color, he made the world more vivid. He was bright and wondrous and while not all knew his name, they knew that they were home in his art, and that was more than enough."

"Hi, Ellie!" Henry Jordan crammed into his seat.

I shifted out of the memory of the pencil drawing of the world you had drawn in sixth grade. I shifted out of feeling like I was writing a story that I could breathe into life.

"Hi, Henry!" It felt safer to look at Henry. He looked happy, as if it was a miracle that I gave him my full attention and another smile. He sat up straighter. He rested his hand on wrinkly jeans, seemed suddenly aware of their crinkliness, and started to smooth his hands over them with no luck.

His eyes slanted toward me and his Adam's apple bobbed as if he was nervous. The more attention I gave to Henry the more annoyed you seemed, shifting in your seat, restless. I decided that "annoyed" suited you very well, so I turned all my attention to Henry and even flashed him a rare smile featuring all of my teeth (I did have good teeth).

You were writing on a sheet of ruled paper, twirling your pencil before scribbling.

Mr. Jameson charged in, papers piled high in his hands. He looked like a man possessed. He reminded me of Ms. Hooper. Not in the possessed kind of way, but in the way that she could just talk about words and look like there were a thousand light bulbs turned on under her skin. He looked lit up.

A folded sheet of paper appeared in front of me. I narrowed my eyes at it. Both boys looked ahead, innocent. But you had had the pencil, so you were clearly the note's author. I opened up the folded sheet.

You smile at Henry. A lot. On the next line, it read, *I guess Ellie Walker has a crush on the new boy. That's original.*

I wanted to bark a laugh. I had said something similar to you when we were eleven and Lily Flores moved into town. I had said it to embarrass you, but this note felt a little heavier than that.

I smiled and wrote a note back on the corner of the page and shoved it toward you. You didn't move, just your eyes glanced down to read it. Jaw clench. I wanted to giggle in my seat.

Who can say no to dimples?

Boys with dimples did look sweet.

My father did not have dimples.

When I got home, I saw a paper folded in my pocket. I hadn't noticed when you put it there, but I knew it could only be you. In my hands was the note I had passed to you when we were in junior high.

> I want a divorce from our
> unholy best friendship.

Under my note was your reply:

> No.

30

August,

The next day, you were standing by my locker, waiting for me. You didn't see me at first. I looked at you and slowed my steps. You were so tall. You were slender and lean and the muscles corded over your arms in a way that made me a little breathless. I had once been wrapped up in those arms when we wrestled as kids, all innocence and toothy grins. I didn't like the surge of feeling when I looked at you. It made me feel sad and excited all at the same time.

You looked up. You didn't smile. You looked vaguely nervous. A little unsure. "Walker, did you get my note?"

I sighed loudly. As if annoyed. I was not annoyed. "Yes, Matthews. I got your note."

"We *did* write 'till death do us part.'"

"We were kids. What do kids know?"

"Lots of things."

"Like . . ."

You bit your lip. "Like maybe a kid knows that he shouldn't have just given up when his best friend pushed him away. That maybe, deep down, he knew he was being a coward when he didn't stick up for her or keep knocking on her door or leaving notes in her locker. That maybe he could have done more to keep his promise."

I blinked.

"And maybe he knows that he will do anything to keep that promise now."

There were so many things that got crammed between us as we were growing up. I was ashamed that the best friend I had ever had started to slip through my fingers because of one afternoon of cowardice. Sure, you had looked away when the kids bullied me or when I was hurting, but it was only because I pushed you away first.

I shifted my weight from foot to foot, grasping for a response. "I am not sure."

"Ellie—"

"I am not sure if I want this kind of commitment, you know? I may stumble upon some other best-friend material and I don't want to get tied down." I held back a smirk.

Fake-angry-glare. "You are such a charming woman."

I looked at my inked-up shoes, lanky legs, and ratty shirt. "I never said I was charming. Neither are you." You

155

were a bottle of charm and I wanted to keep you in my pocket.

I was smiling as I turned toward my next class, but then I felt the color leech out of me and that familiar cold numbness settle in its place. It swept me up when I wasn't looking. It hit when I was midstride. You started chattering on about how you were top grade-A best-friend material, but all I could feel was that I was melting into the linoleum drop by drop and you didn't even see as I dissolved into nothing.

31

Depression,

You always snuck up on me when I wasn't looking. You seeped in and dug in your claws.

Depression can only sink your ship if you let the water inside. I read that in the guidance counselor's office. In a magazine. Neatly tucked between advertisements for Proactiv and Zoloft, you know, the stuff someone puts on their face and in their mouth so that their inside and outside are spick-and-span. But people don't understand that sometimes the boat capsizes. Sometimes the storm pummels the deck like bullets. And there are no life boats or buckets, nothing to toss the water out. Depression, you are the one who took an ax to the wood, you are the one who left the gaping holes where the water rushes in and we don't even remember when you did it. We just wake up and the murky water is pulling us under.

That's how it was.

Waking up in the dark, in the cold, in the wet, but our eyes are already wide open, drinking up summer days and distant laughter and we stare around and wonder how the world could go on oblivious as we stand at its center drowning.

I found the magazine while I was sitting in the guidance counselor's office to discuss plans after graduation. It was hard to think about the future when you were my shadow with the sharpest of teeth, eating me away.

32

Flyer,

I tell my own stories in my head to try to drown out the dark ones. The ones that whisper and prod and clink against my nerves.

I was writing one in my head when a pause in hallway traffic lifted my gaze and I saw you. And like a gunshot, you scared the shadow away. Just for a moment. Just enough. You weren't much. A glossy 8x11 sheet of paper, but I fell in love with you. The picture was of a beautiful campus and bold white columns filling up the entire page.

**CREATIVE WRITING AT
COLUMBIA UNIVERSITY**

I looked at you and felt . . . home.
I felt safe.
I tore you off the wall.
You were all mine.

33

August,

Later that day, I was taping up the flyer inside my locker. I had Googled photos of the campus, I had read and reread the university website over and over again. My fingers lingered over the words. *Columbia University.* The university was prestigious. The flyer seemed to wrap up all my dreams and print it off on an 8x11 sheet of glossy paper. Words like *literary art, vision, creative freedom, power, masterful writers.* Each word was like a lightning bolt splintering into my heart.

In my room, I closed my eyes at night imagining getting the acceptance letter, then taking a backpack and a train out of town up to New York City. I could make it. I knew it. I was so happy that I didn't even care that there was a fresh bruise on my back or that I had heard my momma crying again in the bathroom last night. I would be free! I was counting down the days.

"Earth to Ellie! Earth to Ellie!" You were behind me and I whipped around, too happy to try to ignore you. I had done a good job of that for the past couple of weeks. I wore earphones while in the halls, pretended I was taking notes in class. In Ms. Hooper's class, you didn't sit next to me even though there wasn't assigned seating. You sat a row over and a couple of seats back.

You had started doing that even when we were still best friends. It was around fourth grade. You started sitting in the back and at first it hurt my feelings. I felt like I was losing you, but then you'd gallop up to me right when the bell rang and we would walk to our next class together.

You often tried to do that in Ms. Hooper's class, but right when the bell rang, I would go straight to her desk and ask her about the comments she wrote on my work or what I should look for in a college if I wanted to study writing.

I had found my talisman. Hooper had her books, Jameson had his science, I had Columbia.

You stared at me for a second, a little startled by my lit-up smile.

"Wow . . ."

"What?"

"It's been a long time since I have seen that smile."

"I know where I want to go!" I jabbed a finger at the flyer.

You peered past me to read it.

"Columbia University? New York, huh?"

"Yes!" I was practically at Jameson-level enthusiasm. "I am starting my application now. I want to send it in early."

You looked at me with a soft smile on your face. "Then you'll go."

Your words coaxed my confidence, making it feel possible. There was a pencil tucked behind your ear and a bit of orange paint on your pants and for a moment, I felt sad thinking about you in a suit and tie. I felt sad thinking about a world without your brushstrokes. "You will too."

You blinked. "Me? I'll go to Columbia?"

"You have to tell your parents." I didn't elaborate. I didn't have to because recognition pulled your lips into a small *o* of understanding.

"I just think that . . . if we can, we should try our best to be happy."

You chewed on your lip and looked away from me.

"Tell me right now that you *want* to go to business school. Tell me that and I won't bother you again about it."

You looked at me. You didn't say a word.

34

Depression,

You were a tricky thing. I wanted to be able to scrub you clean and make you shiny so you didn't feel like you were rotting inside of me. I wanted to throw my weight behind you and tip you off the Earth. I wanted to slam my door in your face when you came calling. Sometimes, when I felt strong, I did. I threw you into the basement. I screamed you into submission. I tricked you into the closet. I prettied you up and pretended that everything was all right.

But when you hit and I was unprepared or was already teetering on unsteady legs, I didn't have the lungs to yell, or the weight to shove, or the energy to pretend. You just swept me up and away, so far away. You nibbled on my fingertips and haunted my peripheral vision like a ghost with unfinished business, and that business was me. You hadn't won, and you like to win.

That's why I make worlds in ink, so I can sweep myself away and wish and dream and make believe, and it will feel real for just enough time to let me build up strength again so I can face you and win.

And when I start writing my essay for Columbia, I write all our secrets because on the page, you can't break me.

35

Father,

I sprinted up the steps and sailed right through the front door. I was high on possibility. I wanted to run up to my room and make paper angels out of all the Columbia information that I had printed at school the day before. I was about to pound up the stairs when I heard your voice coming from the living room. "Ellie."

"Yes, Father?" Pleaseleavemealonepleaseleavemealone.

"Come here."

I went into the living room, the smile off my face. I immediately felt small. I immediately felt afraid. I immediately wanted to run.

I stood in silence.

You were sitting with a pile of papers in your hands. You leaned back in your chair. "Do we keep secrets in this house, Ellie?"

"N—no." I shook my head. "No, we don't."

You flipped the stack around and I saw the columns of Dodge Hall and the map of Columbia's campus. You had been in my room.

"Then what are these?"

"Just information on a college."

"This college isn't local."

"I—I know. I just saw it and it has a good program and so I wanted to keep the information. I—I won't be applying." I was lying.

"So you printed over fifty pages of information just for the fun of it?" You started to stand. "Do you think I'm stupid?"

Lighter open. Lighter shut.

"No, I just printed the information."

He nodded, pretending to believe me. "That's good. Because you aren't leaving this house. Ellie, your place is here with your momma and me."

"I know that."

"Good." The lighter lit and you burned the pages.

I turned on my heel and went up the stairs.

36

August,

The night that Father burned those pages, he told me that if I ever tried to break my promise, if I ever tried to leave, Momma would be lonely. "What would happen to her?" he said. Lighter open. Lighter shut. Eyes staring out the window. A threat.

I nodded. I was wrung dry, all the enthusiasm drained out of me. All the dreaming.

The next day when school was done, I ripped the flyer out of my locker and I went to the trash can to throw it in. I was so tired of wanting things and not wanting things, of the rollercoaster of my emotions, of the way everything just felt too far and out of reach.

Maybe it was time to stop reaching, like Momma.

I was shaking, but I finally threw it in. I must've stayed there long after the bell rang, because by the time I looked up, the halls were empty except for you. You watched me with unjudging saucer eyes. My hand fell to my side, suddenly ashamed.

Girls like me shouldn't have big dreams. They stay in their houses of secrets and die there.

I turned around and walked toward the front door of the school. I battled my thoughts all night, wrestling back and forth with the possibility of New York, of Columbia, of classrooms and professors and beautiful stained-oak doors. It seemed like it was galaxies away from my row house on Sunset Street.

The next day, I shuffled in a daze to my locker. I almost didn't notice when the folded sheet fell out. It tumbled onto the floor and landed on top of my shoe. I leaned over to pick it up, eyes narrowed, and unfolded it. Glossy paper. A dream nestled in my hands. On the lower right corner were familiar scratchy letters. "Deadline for admission is in three months. Remember, we can go Anywhere."

You didn't sign it. But I knew it was you. Your penmanship never got much better after fourth grade, which was especially surprising because you drew and painted like someone destined for art galleries. I looked around the halls and couldn't find you, but I searched hastily in my locker for Scotch tape. I held my breath, practically frantic. When I found it, I bit my lip and tore off a piece. Like before, the flyer fit perfectly on the inside of my locker door. Yes, it fit perfectly. My fingers traced over the letters again and I smiled.

I printed off the pages again in the school library.

I hid them in my closet.

37

Momma,

You were working later and later. Father had gotten a job down at the wood mill and his hours were longer too. There were still nights you came home later than him. I didn't know why you'd risk that since that just made Father's beatings worse. He was angry that you were working so much. I ignored your little noises of pain or the shower running to cover your tears late at night.

Not because I didn't care, but because you had made your choices and I refused to make the same ones. I blocked out the world with words. Writing essays for Ms. Hooper. Writing and rewriting and throwing away stories for

Columbia. I kept writing about broken things, secrets, sad things, but something felt wrong with the way the lines fit together. They weren't the stories I wanted to write.

I wrote in the dark while you shook in the shower.

I tiptoed around my house and took the belt beatings whenever Father had too much whiskey and too many excuses for violence, but my bruises would go away.

The ink from my pen would remain.

I wrote even as I put a pillow over my ears so I couldn't hear you cry.

I smooshed myself into the lines and lived there so I could pretend that Sunset Street didn't exist at all.

38

August,

"I told them!" You were running toward me as I sat in a patch of green grass behind the school. Everyone had left and I had been enjoying the heat and the quiet. I raised my hand to block the sun from view and saw you, wild-eyed and grinning. How is there enough space in the world for those big eyes and smile? I couldn't help but smile back even if I had no idea what you were talking about.

Then it clicked. You had told them that you were planning on going to art school.

You were on full blast, like an explosion of color and light, a giddy and breathless expression of joy.

I stand up. "No. Way."

"Yes. Way." You matched my staccato rhythm.

I raised my hand to awkwardly high-five you and you ignored it, leaned in, and wrapped me up in your arms. I sharply inhaled, a little uncertain. But you were warm and buzzing with an energy that barely fit inside the northern hemisphere, let alone your body. It was the biggest hug in the world, and it was mine. I smiled against your soft cotton T-shirt, breathing in the smell of detergent and oil paint.

I didn't realize that we were standing there holding each other with no space between us, until I heard your breath hitch.

My hands were wrapped around your neck, your hands were wrapped around my waist. We were two bodies that were neatly pressed together. When did they get tangled up in each other? Who pulled or yanked our hug into something new and electrifying?

I wondered that as I felt your face lower and your nose lightly brush mine, and I felt your breath hot on my face. You swallowed. Licked your lips. Your breath unsteady.

And then I felt you.

I felt *you*.

I blinked, trying to focus.

You were hard under your jeans.

I blinked again, confused. You want me. Like *that*?

My body was one million pinpricks of delight, of desire,

of blinding exhilaration that made my stomach do flip-flops on its own invisible trampoline. I needed a bungee cord to keep myself tethered to the Earth because I just wanted to float away.

My body was taut—alert—and deep in my belly I felt an ache that twisted but still felt good. Like I was being hollowed out and was swallowing sun-soaked honey all at once. We weren't moving, just feeling the slope and planes of our bodies and the way they were close, too close, but not close enough.

I heard you swallow again and your hands ever so slowly tightened around me. I was a sunflower in your cupped hands and you wanted to kiss my petals without hurting them. I felt that, that hesitation and desire. It rolled off you in waves and crashed over me and I wanted to drink it all in. I curled my fingers into your hair and let my nose graze your neck, and your Adam's apple bobbed under the touch.

"Ellie—I . . ." You suddenly seemed embarrassed by the hardness under your pants and I wondered if I should be too. You stepped back to create space between our legs, but then dipped down so your face was a whisper away from mine. Your lips brushed my cheek and I closed my eyes. You were breath and eyelashes and hands and I leaned into you, hungry. Hungry for things I didn't know or understand, but starving all the same.

"You are holding your breath," you said.

I realized I was. I was holding in all the oxygen, all the air to not disturb the moment, to not ruin it.

"I don't want to blow you away," I said, and I felt your lips curve up into a smile on my neck.

"I am staying right here, Ellie. Always."

And I believed you. Your lips drifted from the curve of my neck, to the edge of my jawline, and then your lips brushed mine with the softest of kisses. A kiss for petals and bruised knees and holy best friendships turned into something new.

We both exhaled. We both leaned back. We both felt the ache, pull, desire, and fragile bright thing between us.

I blinked, because I wanted to hold it.

But I didn't think I could.

I stepped back. I felt like I was falling. Not in a falling-head-over-heels-into-soft-clouds kind of way, but in the nightmare-the-ground-is-about-to-hit-me kind of way. I swallowed. I blinked again. I tried so desperately to shove aside the doubt and reluctance because I wanted to step back into the circle of your arms, but I couldn't.

"Ellie . . ."

"I—I have to go." I didn't want to go, I wanted to stay, but I was afraid that one more touch could ruin everything. One more touch might be a lie.

I turned away from you. The disconnect and the space between us felt like the Grand Canyon had cracked the world in half and we were stumbling apart, and I wanted to cry.

176

"Ellie, I'm sorry, please don't . . ."

I didn't wait to hear what you had to say.

"Ellie . . ." Your voice was louder, more urgent.

I was already running.

You didn't chase me.

39

Momma,

My inked-up shoes pounded the pavement. My mind was a riot of feeling. My body was tearing me in different directions. I wanted to stay near August, I wanted to get closer, but then doubt had solidified into such a real and immovable thing in my chest, and as I ran I remembered what you once told me.

That when you first met Father, it felt like the sky had cracked open and spilled stars around you. That in the beginning, there was nowhere safer than his arms. That a long, long time ago, you were in love with him.

And then you had to cry in showers and whimper in

beds and hide bruises under foundation and too much eye shadow.

I didn't think August would ever hurt me.

But once, you had thought Father would never hurt you either.

Just like how when I saw him on our porch that first time, I didn't know he would bite.

I was scared to give my heart away.

It had already been broken.

I knew how it felt to be stuck in a cage and I was afraid that the circle of August's warm arms could somehow become gnarled iron bars that would trap me in.

I knew because that was your life and you had dragged me into the cage with you and I didn't want to just run into another one.

40

Momma,

You woke me up with a hand stroking my hair. I blinked at you with swollen eyes. I was too tired to get up.

"Are you having a nightmare? You were tossing in your sleep. What's wrong, my dove?"

I was still teetering on dreams. "I don't want to live in a cage."

You stroked my hair again, teasing out the tangles. "You don't belong in a cage."

"But what if . . ." It was dark and I was partly asleep and so I was brave. "Are all men like Father?"

You paused your stroking and inhaled. "No, Ellie. Not

all men are like your father, but you still have to be careful with your heart." The way you said it, it sounded like you meant *Don't be reckless like I was with mine.*

Then you gently put your fingers under my chin. "But that doesn't mean you should close it."

41

Sky,

I was crashing through your clouds without a parachute, plummeting and screaming and the air was sucking up all of the sound. I was flailing my arms, trying to grab onto sunbeams and your cornflower blue, but I was falling, falling, falling and as the ground reached for me, I closed my eyes . . .

And woke up.

42

Dreams,

You were cruel and felt so real and sometimes when I woke up, I still felt like I was falling.

43

August,

　You didn't try to force me to talk to you or push me for an explanation, but after Jameson's class when the bell rang, you were out of your seat like a lightning bolt. In front of me was a folded note. I unfolded it. It wasn't a note at all. It was a drawing.

　It was of our barn bridge. We were kids. We were sitting in the open-air windows, our legs dangling over the edge. My eyes were on the river below, a full-blown smile on my face. I looked happy, alive. I wanted to be that Ellie. The Ellie who breathed in brushstrokes and not the Ellie who felt like she would disappear drop by drop into the floor. Then

I looked at the drawn version of you sitting beside me. Your eyes weren't on the river.

They were on me.

44

Depression,

 I was so tired of the stories of heartache and loss that you kept whispering in my ear. In class, I scratched my nails into the wood desk chairs just to make sure that I was still sitting on them, just to make sure that I wouldn't fall.

 You kept trying to lock me in. But I was slowly finding the key. When I was distracted by college essays and saucer eyes, you got quiet. I was tired of the tender lullabies of goodbye that you whispered in my ear. They sounded so sweet. They also sound like lies.

 And I was tired of the sinking feeling that kept the world so far away.

I was tired of being alone when I knew the world could be just a little brighter.

With him.

So whenever you crept in, I decided to punch back.

To fight.

You didn't belong here anymore.

And that's when I realized what was missing from my story. I pulled out my notebook and I wrote about pain, but I also wrote about hope.

45

August,

I wrote about us.

46

August,

"Hi," you said.

"Hi," I said back.

We were both looking at our feet. My shoes with the words sprawling over the white fabric, your shoes clean. It had been a week since we had actually *looked* at each other. I could feel the hum of energy between us, the pull and anxiety. We were on the sidewalk, but we might as well have been in a broom closet. The air around us felt tight, expectant, uncertain.

"I'm sor—"

"I'm sorry, August." I was still looking at your shoes. "I—I overreacted. It wasn't a big deal and I just, I got . . . nervous."

You were quiet for a moment. "I would never do anything, never try to do anything to hurt you." You stepped closer, shoes closer. I felt your hand lift my chin. You swallowed, and I saw your Adam's apple bob. "Ellie Walker, do you forgive me?"

There was part of me that wanted to say there is nothing to forgive, that I liked to feel you wanting me, that even as I pushed you away, I wanted more of you. Instead I said, "August Matthews, you are forgiven."

You exhaled, and your shoulders slumped in relief. The air around us loosened its grip.

"I mean, what would I have done without the presence of the great August Matthews in my life?"

A smirk. "Suffer. Greatly. Obviously."

"Quite true. It is such a bore to not be incessantly bothered. The silence was maddening."

"Since you are practically Silence's mistress, I will have to call bullshit on that."

"Not true. I have words and worlds bouncing around up here." I point to my temple.

"Yes, but I wish you would use your lips more." You looked at my lips then, one second, two seconds, three seconds.

I wanted to say something, but I was so focused on your eyes looking at my lips that I forgot how to string words together.

Then you shook your head once as if to clear it and stepped back. "Want to go to our bridge?"

I liked how you said "our" bridge. I liked how it had been years since we had been there together, but it was still *ours*.

"Yes, I do."

* * *

The bridge was the same as before. Just older and more used. You walked toward the spot where you'd carved our names in the wood.

I blinked and ran my finger over the letters. "I can't believe it's still so clear."

"It might have had some help." You pulled out the Swiss Army knife from your pocket and twirled it around.

"You've been re-carving it?"

"Maybe."

"Why?"

You shifted from one foot to the other. "I—I didn't want to let you go."

I was blinking fast. I felt awkward and excited and afraid and everything in between.

I stared at your big, huge gray eyes. Those eyes that looked at me and made me feel like I was slipping into them. I stared at you, the boy who raced me down streets and who kissed me on bridges and who drew me pictures that made me feel awake and alive. I wanted to tell you all of this, but instead I blurted out, "Your eyes don't fit in your face right."

You blinked. "My eyes?"

"Yes, they are too big and when you look at me like that I feel like I might trip into them."

"I don't know whether to be flattered or offended." You cocked your head.

"Be offended. Seethe with resentment. Yes, I think that would be most appropriate."

Maybe then I would stop climbing into your eyes, and floating in the gray of them without a lifeboat. I was teetering off balance as I realized that you had the goofiest and most beautiful grin on your face.

"What?" I said, shaking my head clear.

Your eyes and smile seemed to eclipse the whole of your face. You touched my nose. "Maybe I want you to trip into my eyes. I think it would only be fair since I am already lost in your freckles."

My hand flew up to my nose. "My freckles?"

"Do you remember when we were in Ms. Bailey's fourth grade class and we were learning about the stars?"

I narrowed my eyes. "Yes."

You shifted. "I remember looking over at you. I purposely sat behind you and to the side because I wanted to look at you anytime without you filleting me with your gaze. I really loved all my body parts and wanted to keep them."

I smirked and elbowed your ribs. I remembered feeling slighted when you had changed seats. I'd felt like you wanted space. All along, you'd just wanted me to be unaware of your growing attention. I might have blushed.

You smiled and swallowed. "We were learning about stars and how patterns of them had names and when we were playing after school one day, I started to look at your freckles and I wanted to name them like the stars in the sky because I felt like . . . they were beautiful and so far, far out of my reach."

We were quiet. My heart was a bright yellow balloon and was floating somewhere above our heads. You looked away. Like you knew I would get up and leave and you didn't want to see me do it.

"Well, did you ever name"—I made an awkward gesture toward my face—"these constellations?"

I held my breath, certain I would pass out on the buckled-wood bridge floor.

Finally, you looked up at me. "Every single one."

I exhaled. "Liar." I hoped you weren't lying.

The tiniest quirk of your lips. I wanted to shiver as you leaned in closer.

Your fingers grazed the top of my nose and my cheeks, connecting the dots, voice soft as you started reciting names, "Paris and Helena. Tristan and Isolde. Lancelot and Guinevere. Romeo and Juliet . . ."

"All those names are lovers from literature."

You took a shaky breath and then pulled your hand away, blushing. "That's because every one of them was meant to be kissed."

I held my breath. "Tragic lovers," I said. "Those are all tragic love stories . . ."

"Maybe that's because I didn't think that I would get the happy ending I wanted."

My heart wasn't a single bright balloon. No. It was all the balloons in the world, and it was floating up, up, up into the sky.

"I love you, Ellie," you whispered. "I love you and not like a best friend loves their best friend, but . . . more, more than that." You took a deep breath in, knowing you couldn't turn back even if you were afraid of my response and so you charged forward, seemingly emboldened by my silence. "I love the way you smile when you look at blank pages, I love the way you raise your hand in class even when you aren't quite sure of the answer, I love the excitement in your voice when you talk about Columbia, I love the world you built for us when we were kids, I love the way you look at my drawings and see me there, truly see me. I love the way you look at me. I love the way you say my name as if you could fit all the good things of summer into it. I love who you are—inside and outside. I love you, Ellie Walker."

I didn't say anything back to you. You were bursting with nervous energy and I wanted to kiss every inch of you, but I couldn't. Not yet. I soaked in all of you. I did love you, August. I *do* love you. I knew that for so long, but I'd been too afraid to say it.

You reached out to grab my hand. "Ellie, please . . . say something."

I looked at you. The boy who made me forget my house, my secrets, my oceans of unshed tears. The boy who gave me strength to battle my own shadows in the dark.

I was still floating with clouds when I looked at you. "I have a story to tell you." I stood up and brushed off my jeans. "But you'll have to wait till tomorrow." I planted a kiss on your cheek and I ran.

I ran with a smile on my face.

47

August,

We were in Ms. Hooper's class. You were fidgeting by your desk trying to lock eyes with me, but I ignored you. I didn't want to lose my nerve. I walked up to Ms. Hooper and her smile turned on me with its dazzling ferocity. It almost startled me, but I just blinked and whispered, "I'd like to read my story. To the class."

Her smile stretched across her face. "That's wonderful, Ellie! Would you like to read it tomorrow? Fridays are usually when we share—"

"No, can I read it today? Right now?" I bit my lip.

She cocked her head and saw something in my expression

that led her to nod. "Go ahead, Ellie. You can start out class."

She stood up and everyone quieted in their seats and she told the class that I was going to read a story. There were a few snickers, a few chair creaks, but I just took my backpack off my shoulder and pulled out the assignment I had written. The story that I had turned in to Ms. Hooper that had an A-plus across its top. The story I had submitted for my Columbia application.

Ms. Hooper sat. The other students were quiet. I dropped my backpack to the floor and then I built up my backbone, vertebra by vertebra. I always felt like I was cracking open and splintering apart, but in front of everyone, I felt like I was being stitched back together, into place. Like the joints and seams of me finally figured out how to make room for each other so I could stand a little straighter, hands shaking and bones creaking, but my voice strong.

With everyone listening, the sound of me took up all the spaces that felt infinite and inconsequential: the space between me and the stars, the space between my toes, the space between the broken doorjamb and the door, the space between Ms. Hooper's sparkling eyes and my two hands, the space between me and you.

You watched me, but I didn't meet your gaze. I was afraid that if I did, I wouldn't be brave enough to read the words written on my page.

"There once was a boy made of color and brushstrokes,

and one day he met a shadow wobbling on shaky legs beside him and he decided to paint her beautiful . . ."

And then I told our story. Without our names. Without this town. I told a story of swords and sorrow and secrets. I told of a shadow who learned to breathe and a boy who learned to paint the world bright and new.

The only three words I didn't say were *I love you*. But every word had those three crammed between them. *I love you* was swinging from every syllable and hanging off every letter. *I love you* was whispered in every single line.

And when I finally finished and looked up to see you, your eyes were open and your lips were smiling and I knew that you had heard every single one of them.

48

Father,

I walked home and I felt like I was riding wishing flowers as I skipped over cracks in the cement. Every cell sizzled with effervescent giddiness. I was quite sure that I could become intoxicated on this feeling.

But any high only lasts for so long.

The feeling was doused by your anger when I got home.

You found my college application that day. I had spent months filling it out. I had printed it so I could scribble in the margins and write notes on the forms in the middle of the night. Making sure they were all just right.

You didn't read them. You just took out your lighter and burned every page.

You locked Momma out of my room and beat me with your belt until it broke the skin.

I cried, but *I* didn't break.

And even as the slaps of the belt hit and I bit down on my lip till it bled and Momma cried from behind the door, I wanted to smile at you.

I had already read my story aloud. It was in the world. Infinite. Immortalized. August had heard it.

And that paper application you burned? It had just been for practice for when I had to fill it out online.

I had clicked send on it the day before at school.

You were already too late and you didn't even know it.

Later that night, my back was too sore from the beating to lie on it. I was exhausted, so I fell asleep sprawled out on my mattress. I still wanted to smile, but sleep claimed me.

I couldn't be sure, but in between dreams, I thought my eyes opened to see Momma at the foot of my bed with her head in her hands.

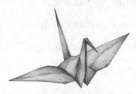

49

Momma,

I saw you in the kitchen the next morning.

"How can you stay with him?" I said. "Can't you see what he is?"

You were quiet at first, but then said, "Of course I can."

"Then why—"

"Because . . . Because . . ." Your voice was tired and uncertain.

"Because what!" I practically shouted over the counter, and your hands paused on the frying pan.

You looked up at me. "Because sometimes you don't have a choice."

I stared at you. There was always a choice.

You hunched your shoulders. "He doesn't try to be the way he is. He just doesn't know how to hold anything he can't control, anything that is too real."

He never saw the me that was real.

Although that wasn't entirely true. He did see me. The me that was like the old you.

The me who wanted to be free.

You kept us in this box, these bars disguised as walls.

Once we ruled from a throne on a mountaintop. Once you were a queen.

That was so, so long ago.

I leaned away from the counter and turned toward the door. "You are making excuses for him, Momma. We should've just left years ago."

"We will. Ellie, I—"

"I don't want to hear it, Momma."

I'd listened to enough lies in my head.

I wasn't going to listen to yours.

50

August,

I didn't go to school on Friday. I was all bruises and butterflies. The black and blue peeked out above what my oversize T-shirts could hide and my stomach fluttered with emotions. I wanted to see you. Even if the thought of seeing you made me feel anxious.

I spent my afternoon and evening with pictures of Columbia spread out across my floor. Father hadn't found them. I dared to look at them even when he was in the house. My fingers grazed over the classical architecture, the columns, and the beautiful red brick. There were so many photos that the printer at school had run out of color ink and the last few photos were a mishmash of black, white, and color.

It didn't matter. Sitting in the middle of all the photos, I felt *there*. I was one of the blurs with a backpack stepping into Dodge Hall. I was someone who belonged amid pillars, and stone, and green patches of grass where I could sit and think beside a bronze casting of Rodin's *Le Penseur*. I didn't hear the loud TV down the hall, or feel the soreness of my ribs, or think about the fact that I was sitting in a house with cracked and peeling walls where I locked my room at night.

I was there.

Not here.

And I was happy.

I picked up each photo like they were pieces of gold and tucked them away. I would take photos of my own soon. Very soon.

I fell asleep smiling.

* * *

Hours later I heard a *tat-tat-tat!* The tapping on my window woke me up and I shot up, bolt straight. I jerked my gaze to my door and heaved in a breath. Still locked. I looked at my window. Had it been the wind? The tree? I never realized how close the nearby branch came curling toward my window.

Tat-tat-tat! Rocks. Little rocks were being tossed at my window. I narrowed my eyes before throwing off my blankets and running to the window. I stared out of it and held my breath, and there you were.

Your smile was wide as you perched on that branch. With a handful of rocks, you looked like you were twelve years old. I opened my window and stuck my head out, whispering, "What the hell do you think you are doing?"

"You can't read a story like that and then not show up for school the next day. You practically torpedoed out of class yesterday and then you avoided me the rest of the day."

"I wasn't trying to avoid you." I absolutely had been trying to avoid you.

"I was on the verge of literal heart failure."

"Doubtful." I leaned against my window frame. "Besides . . . patience is a virtue."

"I'm not very virtuous."

I smiled. "I noticed." I swallowed and then looked back into my room. "You should go."

"Come out with me."

"Are you crazy?"

"Please. I need to show you something."

"August, I can't leave my house."

"Oh, c'mon. Live a little." You reached out your hand and pointed to the lattice. "We don't have to stay out long."

I leaned out the window. It did look sturdy, it did seem easy, it did sound like an adventure that felt like the first of many.

I shifted my gaze back to you and grinned but when

I did, your smile was gone, your eyes were wide, and you stared at me. I blinked, confused.

Then I saw your eyes taking in the whole of me. In my tank top. With all of the bruises blooming over my skin.

I stepped back into my room's shadows. I felt naked, ugly. I felt like all the balloons that had my heart soaring were popping at once. *You saw me. The real me. The parts of me that are broken.* "August, leave." I grabbed the top of the window and started to pull it shut, to shut you out—

—and you reached out and stopped the window from closing. "Ellie."

"Just go."

"What happened?"

"August . . ." The sadness hit me like a tidal wave. The ferocity of it gripped me by the throat. "Just go," I said through clenched teeth.

"Ellie Walker. Please don't shut me out. Please. Tell me what happened."

And even as I felt like I was clawing for breath and dragging myself out of the torrent of whispers and despair, I realized I wanted to tell you. I wanted to tell you everything.

"Ellie, please." Your voice broke.

"We aren't twelve anymore. We can't go around playing make-believe or slaying imaginary monsters. There are real monsters in this world. And"—I pointed to the branch—"you are going to break that branch!" I was so close to the cool night air and to you. My eyes were on the sky, my feet were on the warped hardwood floor.

"I once heard a story about how a boy of paint and a girl of ink could slay any monster together. The *real* monsters." Your eyes looked glassy in the moonlight. "The ones you never tell me about."

Together. I inhaled the night air. I leaned over to grab a long-sleeve shirt so that the bruises would be hidden. I was going to *tell* you everything, I didn't want to force you to *see* everything.

"Don't hide them, Ellie," you whispered. "Don't hide them from me anymore."

I clutched the long sleeve in my fist. *Hide. Hide. Hide.* That's all I wanted to do, but your voice was feather-soft and it tickled that part of me that wanted to be seen.

"Okay."

I dropped the long-sleeve shirt to the ground, and while it didn't make a sound, I felt like it crashed like smashing glass.

I pulled my leg over the windowsill and found purchase in the small holes of the lattice. I heard you climb your way back down the tree. I felt the wood between my fingers and felt every steady step on the way down. As I looked up, the distance between me and my window growing, I wondered how I never saw my window as an escape route before.

My feet touched the grass and it was cool and dewy. I closed my eyes, fingertips still clinging to the lattice as if letting go would break me.

Your hands went to my shoulders and I felt the warmth

of you step closer. You leaned down and whispered in my ear, "Let go, Ellie. You can let go."

And I did. Weaving your fingers through mine, we ran.

It was our special place in the woods. I knew that. It had lived on and grown without us, becoming more wild and beautiful as I was locked away and rotting. What I hadn't expected were the candles. Battery-operated candles were everywhere, making our little childhood space look magical once again.

Did you know that I wouldn't be able to see the magic without them? I looked at you, and you sheepishly looked back. "I wanted you to see it like I see it."

Your hand was rough and callused, but you hadn't let go yet. I pulled free so that I could step into our land of dragons and castles, our little world of victories and magic. I turned in a circle. The electric candles flickered like real flame and I smiled. "Electric candles?" I asked.

"What? You think I was going to risk burning down our childhood home with real flame all for the sake of a romantic setting?"

"So, is this supposed to be romantic?" I felt strange asking. It felt too intimate.

"It . . ." You looked around and shrugged as color flooded your cheeks. "It's . . . for you. For us. I—I don't want to say anything more about it because I think . . . you might run away from me. Again." Your eyes shone in the darkness and flickering orange. "Like always."

"I wish this was real," I said, motioning around.

"It was. It was all real." You stepped forward, careful to not trod on the plastic lights, and reached for my hands. My heart thudded in my chest and I hesitated looking up at you. You cupped my cheek.

"What we had here was real. You shut me out. You didn't let me in." You let go of my hands and I let your fingertips trail up my arms to rest on my shoulders lightly where the bruises bloomed in rotting colors. "Why didn't you tell me? Why couldn't you let me save you?" You were so very close. "Why couldn't you let me be your knight in shining armor for once, just for once?"

I could feel the tears coming, feel the sob building like a volcano, and I didn't want to cry.

"Because you aren't my knight in shining armor. You're my boy of painted dreams," I whisper. "I was too afraid to ask you to paint me as someone new, someone different. I was too afraid to ask you to paint all of my pain away. I was too afraid to ask you to paint me unbroken." And then I told you everything. It felt a little bit like loss, and a lot like freedom.

You looked at every bruise. You saw me and your eyes were sad. "Ellie, you might be hurting, but you were never broken."

I wasn't going to sob, going to bawl. Not there. Not with you. Not after keeping it all in for so long. I couldn't break now. I pulled away and stepped to leave, but your hand snaked out and grabbed me and yanked me against your chest. You were so warm, solid.

"Let me go!" I said, wriggling to get free, desperate to flee before the tears came.

"No," you said. "No." You held me so close and so tight that I felt as if you were the stone walls, the tall fortress where Momma and I were once queens and warriors, and I didn't need to keep my own walls up anymore, because I simply couldn't. I collapsed against your chest, burying my face in your shirt, and the cries spilled out—loud, wet, and aching. I couldn't stop.

You held me while I let the tears inside flood out and you kissed the very places that I had spent a lifetime keeping secret.

With each hiccupping breath, you just held me tighter and whispered, "I am here. I will always be here."

I don't know how long I cried in your arms. I don't know when you pulled me into your lap, sitting on the ground. I don't know the precise moment when you started to kiss me.

But you did. It was a soft, light brush of lips on my shoulder where my skin was ugly and ruined and yet you kissed me there anyway. My breathing was quieter, my cries gone. I was spent and tired and could feel a dull headache at my temples.

You kissed my shoulder and then looked at me.

Is this okay? your eyes asked—no expectation, no pressure.

My eyes must have said yes, because you kissed my shoulder again. Then brushed your lips up my neck, until your forehead was resting on mine and our breaths danced together in the dark. Your hand, your long artist's fingers, grazed the skin at my waist. Your breath hitched as you kissed me. "Ellie, I love you . . ."

"I love you too."

I felt you, the wanting in you, pressed up against me. Your head was cradled between my shoulder and neck, your lips brushing my skin there. My pulse was a riot and my skin was on fire and I wanted to implode.

Self-conscious about what you knew I could feel against my thigh, you angled your hips away from me, creating distance, but I didn't want distance. I didn't feel dirty, or used up, or like something was being taken from me. Every touch and kiss felt like something was being given back to me, between gasping breaths and arched backs, I felt like I could just be there, in your arms, loving you and you loving me and the stars and trees as our witnesses. I wanted them to witness it all.

I pulled you down among the flickering candles, I pulled you down on top of me, so that I felt your entire weight balanced above me. You were poised between my legs and propped up over me. We had jeans and T-shirts and buttons and zippers separating us, but this felt more intimate than anything I had seen in the movies.

You said my name again, looking into my eyes. I rocked

my hips against you, wanting more, needing more, and you shivered, your breath unsteady. I kissed you, kissed you until you were gasping and moving on top of me until we were both breathless. My hand moved up under your shirt and I felt the strain of your back and shoulder blades and the skin slick with sweat. I licked you just to see what your skin tasted like. You made a low, rumbling, hungry sound. You kissed my jaw, then my temple, then my neck.

"Ellie, you make me feel like I am floating even when my feet are on the ground." Your heart was floating on balloons too.

I looked into your eyes, your sweet, big, beautiful eyes. "You make me feel awake, alive, you chase the sad thoughts away. You draw me and I feel like I am whole. Like . . . I am beautiful."

"Ellie, you are whole. These"—you brushed your fingers over my bruises, over my scars—"don't make you less. I just want to keep you safe."

You held me, and in your arms, I didn't feel chipped away or like glass about to shatter. You were a man who didn't have to ruin things to hold them. You held me and I felt stronger.

"I don't want to have to be kept safe," I said. "I just want to not be afraid." I just wanted to be free. With you.

Your eyes were wet. "Don't be afraid of me."

"I'm not. Not anymore."

I took off your shirt and then you took off mine and

then we were nothing but two bodies holding each other in the dark.

Two bodies feeling and knowing each other for the first time.

Two bodies who weren't afraid.

I felt you and all I could think about was how you once named all the constellations on my face. I felt like I was a bright and wondrous and wild thing, just like the stars and the paint on your canvas.

51

Momma,

Everything felt more vivid, more real, more alive and awake and buzzing. August was holding my hand and pulling me closer, stealing kisses. We knew all of each other. He had been soft and gentle and for a sliver of time, I felt like we were the subjects in one of his paintings. In a world painted new.

It was still dark, but in a few hours dawn would break. I kissed him goodbye despite his protests to stay by his side. I wanted our time together to be unblemished by reality, or the reality I had always known. He watched me go and then turned toward his house, but every few strides, he looked back at me, a smile on his face.

I didn't hear the shouting until I got to the lattice ladder outside of the house. I peered in the window. The lights were on in the kitchen and living room. Father had your arms braced against the doorway in a vise-like grip. You looked like you were praying for the world to stutter to a stop so that you could walk off it. "Where is she?"

She. He knew I'd left. How could he have known? They had been sleeping when I snuck out with August. I was huddled in the shadows watching as you shook your head. "She's spending the night at a friend's house, she's . . ."

He *SLAPPED* you hard across your face so that it whipped to one side. You held your cheek.

"Her door was locked, Regina," he said in that quiet and terrible way. "From the inside." He pulled a chair out and sat in front of you so that he was looking up into your eyes. "And her window is open." He pinched your chin between his thumb and forefinger. He made you look at him. "Do you think"—he brought his face closer to yours—"that I am a fucking fool?"

"No," you whispered, breathless. "No, of course not. I thought . . ."

"You thought wrong." He grabbed your hair and dragged your face even closer to his lips and they brushed your cheek. I didn't hear what he said. The words were too quiet.

I stared in through the window. If someone were to watch you and Father in slices, if they zoomed in, if they cut out all the noise or edited out the things they didn't want to see, they could almost look in the window and see passion and not pain, they could almost think that my father was just pulling his wife in closer, because he wanted to feel her closer, not because he wanted to use her up.

I blinked away tears. That's when I noticed that you were dripping wet. Your hair and your shirt were soaked. Like you'd stepped into the shower stream with all of your clothes on. You were shaking. And behind you, I saw the gas can.

The lighter was in Father's hand.

I ran to the door and flung it open. "Momma!" The house smelled like gasoline.

Father's gaze shifted to me slowly and he tilted his head. "I told you, Ellie. I told you what would happen if you didn't stay."

You started to pull away, but I could see his grip on you. I could see how you were shaking. I thought you would shake to pieces. "Ellie," you said, and I saw you mouth the word as father's eyes stayed locked on mine. *Run.*

Father clicked open the lighter. And let the flame blaze to life.

I wasn't going to run away. I charged forward and grabbed the lighter out of his hand before the flame hit the gasoline. It burned my palm. He tried to grip my arm, but I was already running back toward the door and I flung the lighter as far as I could into the dark. His lighter was the only flame in the house. There were no matches.

I thought he would run outside to look for the lighter, and I readied myself to lock him out when he did, but instead he slammed the door shut and dragged me by my hair along with you. We were scared, but emboldened by each other, we both struck out trying to scratch and claw at him. But he just threw us to the ground and then started kicking. We clung tight to each other, both of us wrapping our arms around the other's head to shield the blows.

I could feel the magic that lived in the night only hours before crack and break to pieces along with bones.

I don't remember passing out, but before I did, I thought about the bruises under your makeup. I thought about our house that kept so many secrets. I thought about how you once tried to run away and he found you. I thought about how I'd never be able to leave. I thought about how nowhere would want me anyway. I thought about the dreams I had and they all slipped from my grasp as I faced the reality:

I would never get away.

Neither would you.

52

Depression,

Momma and I clung tight to each other that night and when I woke up, we were both bloody and on the floor, tangled up in our pain and secrets.

And you returned, fierce and incessant, and I had nothing left to fight back.

You won.

the last day

53

Life,

It was a Monday. I was supposed to meet August at school. I was supposed to talk to Ms. Hooper about my final creative piece.

But I didn't do any of that. Instead I waited until Momma and Father left for work.

I had already decided my fate, and unlike all of the times before, the thought was a solid thing that wouldn't shove off my chest. It clouded every inch of my mind and I felt like I was a robot moving through a script that was coded in me. I saw myself go through the motions, saw each step as it played out in my head, and it all made me feel this wave of relief.

I knew what I would do. I'd thought about it all week-end. I'd prepared. I'd slept in my shoes because I knew I would miss them and I knew I couldn't take them with me. My shoes were years of Sharpied hopes that now felt like lies.

Sunday night, I fell asleep staring at the ceiling beam in my room. Other thoughts fought their way in—thoughts of flour fights, and kisses near electric candles, and hope taped to the inside of a locker, but there was none of that left. There was just me and the thought of my impending escape.

Father never found his lighter in the backyard, but I did.

***

On Monday, the sky was blue and the sun was glaring. I waited till I heard the roar of the Cadillac drive away. I went to my closet and pulled out the papers on Columbia and the story I'd read for August.

I wrote stories so that I could live in them. But they weren't magic after all.

I took the battery out of the fire alarm. I put all the papers in a metal bowl that Momma had picked up from an old antique shop years ago. Back when we still could laugh loudly in our kitchen and make messes, back when we had no Cadillac in our driveway.

I took everything that meant anything and put it in the metal bowl. I lit it on fire with Father's lighter. He was always destined to burn our lives to the ground anyway.

I watched as the papers crinkled into ash, blackening at the edges. I swallowed hard, smelling it as it burned. I watched till every page turned to dust.

Death would be my escape. Maybe it would be kind. I was waiting for the peace. The quiet. The relief.

None of it ever came.

I thought that if I remembered the night when the world was bright and new and cloaked in candlelight and unbroken things, that it would be enough to say goodbye.

It wasn't.

now

54

August,

The torrent of memories fades away.

You slept in our candlelit grove. You shook from tears and tossed and turned and roared and cried some more. You are awake now, tossing and turning, with your arms wrapped around your middle. The tears you cry now, I will never forget. I sit next to you and pretend that I can feel your shoulder underneath my head.

We stay like that until dawn. Your fits of tears coming and going, but my name is a mantra that you never stop saying.

It isn't until the sky is full of light, orange, yellow, and shining on your face, that I see something new in your eyes. You start running. We pass by houses and broken sidewalks. Your feet move so fast. There is urgency and desperation in every step. I can't pretend to use the pavement to propel me forward. I have to glide in my unearthly way to keep up. It takes me a while to figure out where you are going, but then it clicks as I see the factory ahead.

I trail you, desperate to pull you back. *Don't go there. Not there.* But that is exactly where you are going. Toward the one person that I don't want you to see.

You charge on. I begin to see all of your flaws. All the ways you are still a boy and not yet a man. All the ways you still need someone to protect you. I want to shove a world between the two of you, because every step you take closer to *him* is a step closer, I am afraid, to you being beaten and bruised.

The men beside him notice you first. They narrow their eyes and then take a curious step back. Then he turns around, and I freeze. He's wearing that cool look, the one that comes before a punch or a threat.

"And why are you here?" he says.

"This . . ." You don't stop walking. You just charge forward. I barely see when you cock your arm back. ". . . is for Ellie."

The punch slams my father's face to the side with a loud crack. My father stumbles back, shocked. He stands upright. "Watch your step, boy—"

"Or what?"

"Or I'll beat you till your momma doesn't even recognize you."

The men beside him laugh. My father glances behind him to chuckle along, but I can hear the edge in it. You plow into him, grabbing his flannel shirt and pushing him back against the metal siding of a truck. My father goes for a punch, but you are so fast that he misses you. You don't miss his jaw. Not the first, second, or third time. I stare in awe. You look too lean, too young, too sweet to leave a man bleeding, but you do.

My father slides to his knees and spits out blood. "You are gonna regret that."

"I hope you have bruises."

"What?" he asks, sputtering.

"I hope you are covered in black and blue bruises. I hope that every goddamn person sees them. You won't be able to hide them, cover them up." You lean down and punch again.

Father is wheezing.

I'm unsure if I like how there is blood on your knuckles or that the blood is his. Unsure if I like how you are much stronger than I ever imagined or that he is so much weaker.

But I do know this: I like watching you as you walk away, blood on your hands, sweat on your brow, and my father lying in the dirt.

* * *

229

You walk to my house and stand in front of it. Momma isn't there.

You stare up at the house. Your eyes are red. You chew on your lip and then pull something out of your pocket and write on it. Before I can see what it is, you drop it in the mailbox.

The mailman is right behind you and you almost plow into him when you turn around. He says hello, but you just nod and make your way down the steps.

I watch you leave, but now that I know everything . . . I have to go back and face what's left.

55

Momma,

I wait for you in the living room. I want to see you. I am amazed how much I want you to hold me. How much I miss the warmth of you.

You walk in the door and drop your purse on the couch. Your face is painted, but your brown eyes are dull and empty. There is a pile of mail under your arm. I breathe in deeply, waiting for you to sit down, but you never do. You drop the mail on the counter and start looking in the refrigerator for dinner ingredients. I want to see what August left in our mailbox.

You click the answering machine and a single message

plays: "Hello, Mrs. Walker." You flinch as you let the message play and walk over to pull out the dishes from the cabinet. "We are waiting to hear from you on how you would like to present your daughter's body during the memorial service. It appears you haven't chosen a date or a casket yet and I wanted to let you know that it is important to make this choice today as the . . . well, her body, um . . . please call me so we can make proper arrangements to honor her."

You let a dish clang in the sink. I jerk my head toward you, thinking you must've dropped the pot in, but then another clang comes as you throw another pot into the sink. You are shaking.

The message beeps off and you exhale as you put some water in one of the pots. You bring it to our stove and set it down on one of the two electric burners that still work and stare into the water.

What are you thinking? Your eyes slowly travel to the pile of mail. You always stood over the trash can when you opened the mail because such a huge amount of it was either advertisements or collection letters. You assume the position and one by one you throw them in the trash until your hand freezes. I look over your shoulder.

You are holding a photograph in your hands.

Your fingers tremble as you smooth it out. It is crumpled, but it is me. The one that was tacked up on August's wall. Just like August's, your finger brushes the photo as if you can brush my hair behind my ear. You kiss the photograph.

"Oh, Ellie. I haven't seen that smile in so long. I wish—" You break off in a hiccupping breath.

You flip it over and I see August's handwriting.

The girl I love.

The girl who left.

The girl we will remember.

She once told me that you have freckles just like her. . . .

I hope the world gets to see them.

You inhale slowly and press the photograph to your heart. You wipe the tears from your eyes. Sniff and steady your breathing. You are looking around the room and then back to the photograph. You nod once, kiss the photo, and reach for the phone. Slowly, you dial each number with your index finger. Swallowing hard, you lean against the door-jamb. I hear when the receiver on the other end picks up.

"Yes, hello," you say into the phone. "I—I have figured out the arrangements for my daughter."

I kiss your forehead the way you used to do to me when I was little. You keep your words steady, and when I look into your eyes, I think I see it. The light that should have been there is back. It might not look like hope, but it does look like strength.

You run upstairs and start scrubbing your face clean. You scrub until your skin is splotchy and red, but you don't stop until there is nothing left to disguise you. No doll face. You tear through your room, pick up clothes, and shove them into your bag along with money. Money you hid away over the years, in shoes, in small boxes, in every nook and cranny. Our house was a box of secrets—if only you'd had someone to tell them to.

I watch as you brace yourself in front of my door, looking in.

The horror of it hits me. The moment you unlocked the door and opened it, the seconds that passed when you saw your daughter dead, stealing all your breath and hopes along with her. The daughter that you had lunged to save from belt beatings and whose door you would quietly lock from the inside; who you drove to the mountains and who you dreamed of flying away with like the two small birds you hid under her mattress.

I fall to my knees beside you in the hallway. *What have I done?*

You step over the threshold. One foot, then the other. Your hands lightly brush over every piece of furniture in the room before you stand in the spot where you found me. You touch everything tenderly and hold it to your chest. Plucking through my things with such care, nothing like the way you hurled your belongings into your bag.

Your glassy eyes are so vibrant and suddenly I understand.

Ms. Hooper had her books as her talisman.

Mr. Jameson had his science.

August had his art.

I had Columbia.

You had me.

Tears claw at my throat. It burns and aches. You put my notebooks, my broken teddy bear, my small pillow, and my inked-up shoes in your bag.

You walk toward the door. Back straight and eyes shining. You don't look behind you.

56

Momma,

The roar of the engine growls in the driveway, but you stand there. Face clean of makeup, eyes full of tears. You don't run to the bathroom for your concealer. You are unraveling and used up and aching and you don't care if he sees.

I stand beside you as you walk down the stairs with the bags in your hands. You put them behind the couch. You keep my photo in your hands, clutching it as if you could pull me out of it and into the world. You can't—you know that. I see it in the way your chest shakes even as your thumb gently passes over my brow.

The screech of the front door. The footsteps.

We both take a breath in.

And wait.

He's silent, standing there, but as always, we feel him like he has sucked up all the air in the room. Slowly, you look up at him. He is bruised too. His lip is cut, the blood scabbing over. His left eye is starting to turn a shade of blue.

It suits him.

There is electricity in the room, I can feel it. Like a thunderstorm brewing and tinging the air with a warning. I feel the rumble, I feel the crackling. You stare at each other. Your eyes are wet, but your back is straight and you do not look away. Your eyes are roaming over his face, over all the cut and marred bits of him.

Your secret eyes are alive and sparking with their own fire.

Alert and focused, ready.

I take a shaky breath. *Oh, Momma. Please, please, don't.*

Father isn't used to seeing your eyes stare him down like this.

He cocks his head. "You don't look quite right," he says slowly.

Your bark of laughter is a thundercrack. "Oh, Abel. No, it is you. . . . You don't look quite right. Or maybe . . ." you say, tilting your head to the side, "Maybe this is how you were supposed to look all along."

He rubs his hand across his mouth and down his jaw as if he could wipe the bruises off, but he can't. He just re-splits his lip and blood trickles down his chin. There is even a swipe of blood on his hand, dripping onto the hardwood floor.

Shoulders squared, one eye dark with bruises, you say, "I want you out of my house."

His jaw clenches and unclenches; I see the tic of the muscle. I know the time bomb is tick, tick, ticking along with it. He finally yanks the door closed and steps closer, predatorily. "What-did-you-say?"

"I said, get out." You are terrified, but you say the words anyway.

"This is my fucking house, Regina." Slow, lazy, deceitfully unthreatening steps with words low and even, as if he were whispering a sonnet.

"Get out or I will leave."

In a blink, he clears the distance between you, and his hand is wrapped around your throat. "Now, I know I heard you wrong, Regina." He whispers, lips brushing against your ear. "You are mine." One hand still around your throat, he brushes your hair out of your eyes with his other hand. "And you will never"—he levels his gaze on you, as if he is about to kiss you or punch you, it is hard to know which—"never leave."

He shakes you by the throat, just once, nuzzles your ear, and lets go. "Now, get me my dinner." He gives you a quick once-over. "And clean up your face. I don't want to be staring at a street-whore lookalike while—"

"You know what I realized, Abel," you say, cutting him off. "You need me." Your breathing is fast and unsteady. You are bracing yourself. "But I don't need you. I have never needed you." Your voice is rising, it is taking up the room, it is sucking all the air back to where it belongs. "You chased me because I was the only one who was brave enough to leave. You chased me because you didn't like feeling like a fool. You chased me because you needed someone to break and you knew I was too afraid of what you might do to Ellie, to me. I should have left you years ago. I should have bashed your fucking car to bits when I saw it in our driveway."

Father's eyes narrow, his chin leans down, and it feels like a hound has just caught your scent and is ready to attack. "Try it, bitch. I dare you."

The phone, the one we never use, the one that rarely rings, sits between you. You eye it, take a breath, and lunge for it. Father lunges for you too. And you are running around to the other side of the living room, slamming into the back door. Your fingers are dialing.

9-1-1.

You shove all your weight against the door, "Hello, Hello? I have an emergency . . ." You start to scramble away from the door, but Father grabs your arm, flips you around, and the punch sounds like it has cracked every bone in your face and you fall to the floor, the phone still in your hand.

"You little bitch, you . . ."

You are on your hands and knees, crawling. Blood is dripping down your nose. "My husband is beating me," you say into the receiver.

Father pries your hand with the phone away from your face. He slams his boot down, breaking the speaker. You scream. You scream so loud that you could splinter the house into pieces. You've never screamed. You've always choked the sobs down, stayed quiet. You let the studs and floorboards be the only ones who could hear the pain. But now you are screaming and you are crawling for the front door.

I am trying to drag him away from you, but my fingers meet nothing but air.

He takes your shoulders and flips you over, and pins you to the floor underneath him. "You are mine, do you hear me? You belong in this house, you belong with me, and I would rather have you in one million fucking pieces than outside that door so you are going to calm down, shhhhhh, shhhhhh, you are going to calm down and we are going to pretend that none of this ever happened. Okay?" Father's mouth is on your bloody lips.

You are on the floor, on your back, and he thinks he has won. But he doesn't see the light in your eyes, the secret nestled there. You aren't done fighting.

You bite his lip, then knee him in the groin and his hold on you is lost as you shove him away and bolt for the door. He is on your heels and grabs at your feet and he trips you with one strong arm.

You kick at him, launch to your feet, and heave your weight toward the door. The floorboards creak. He swipes again. His hand meets air.

Father is seething and scrambling to his knees.

That's when you stumble across the threshold and the sun, stark and bright, hits your face.

That's when you leave our house of secrets, and lies, and bruises behind.

That's when the sirens, flashing red and blue, pull into our driveway right behind the Cadillac.

57

Father,

    The police take you away.

    Momma won't lie for you anymore.

    You might have wrecked our lives, but yours will burn down along with them.

    And you won't even need your lighter to do it.

58

August,

It only took a day for my body to be cremated. My ashes are in a white urn. It is too white. Too crisp and bright and new, and Momma knows it.

Momma carries a box to your house, sets it down and knocks on your door. She has a tear in her lip, a bruise on her cheek, but her back is straight and when no one answers, she knocks again.

That's when she hears your feet pound down the stairs and sees you fling open the door. Her gaze is steady. Your chest is rising and falling—your eyes searching her face.

Momma's sweet, honeyed voice says, "She really did have the most beautiful freckles, didn't she?"

The words crack the dam between you, and in the span of a breath, you collide in a hug. You hold each other closer. You hold each other up.

When Momma pulls away, your eyes are red and your faces are streaked with tears.

"I have a favor to ask you," she says.

"Anything," you say.

Momma picks up the box she had set down and takes out each item, one by one.

My white urn.

My Sharpied shoes.

Our two old origami doves.

And my old, dried-out gold pen.

"This is how I want to remember her. This—"

"Wait, just wait one sec . . ." You dash back into your house and a few moments later, I see my face in stars on your canvas. "This is how I want to remember her," you say.

Momma runs her fingers over the brushstrokes. "I knew it." She smiles, as bright and vast as the starry night sky. "I knew you were the person who could see her. Like I do. I knew you were the person I needed."

She picks up the urn and holds it to her chest before stretching out her arms to give it to you. "Will you paint her story?"

59

Momma,

As you get into your car, you stare at our house. "This day was supposed to be for us, Ellie," you say, turning on the engine.

I watch as the familiar setting fades. The boarded-up windows. The potholes. The sidewalk cracks.

We drive to the mountains. The urn is on the passenger seat, my seat—all of me nothing but ashes. I sit in the back seat like when I was little, looking at your chocolate eyes in the rearview mirror.

The urn was white, but August made it mine. He took his paints and made me into stars and color, the words from my Sharpied shoes dancing in the sky along with the soaring origami birds. That was how the people I loved saw me. That is what I needed to see.

The moment that August handed the urn to Momma, I felt myself slipping away. I couldn't save anyone. I couldn't fix anything. I couldn't use my two incorporeal hands. I could only see: the pain I dealt, the promises that had been waiting, the ones who loved me and saw my heart as something beautiful even when I couldn't.

We drive away.

I always liked our drives—the wandering, the possibility, the adventure within them. And as I watch the sun glint off the mirror and into your eyes, I know that this will be our last one.

We arrive at Blue Moon Mountain and you park the car off Sunrise Trail. Your shoulders are shaking as you clutch the urn and two ripped and fading paper birds to your chest.

There it is: our fortress. Our castle that we fought for on our last drive to the mountains when you were a queen and I was a warrior.

You exhale loudly before setting the two birds on the stone ledge side by side.

The trees part to show a valley of farms at the foot of the mountains. Patches of green. There is a breeze that blows your hair into your brown eyes.

My ashes are tucked against your chest. Your voice

shakes, but it is real. The tears aren't being suffocated by pillows and no one here will hurt you.

"We were locked in a box for so long, I didn't want to bury you in one."

Now your hands are shaking too. You slowly open the urn and let my ashes fly in the wind.

And then, you sing.

It catches me off guard to hear your voice tremble and rise on the breeze.

You sing about two birds with torn wings who still could be free. It is beautiful and terrible all at the same time. An ocean of unsaid words, of secrets, of whole hearts and whole truths and no room for lies, an undercurrent of pain that could seize and drown the whole world. And even when your voice shakes and breaks, you still sing.

The notes fall on one another just like August's music and I wonder if it is because grief feels like falling, like a rug being yanked from under you and you don't even brace for the fall because you want it to hurt.

The words clink and fall and fly together in your voice and all your words are for me. The words you kept hidden under my mattress, the words I wanted to hear, the words that were always mine.

We are birds with paper wings. Just because the wings were tattered, doesn't mean they could never fly. It doesn't mean that their little fragile lives were worth nothing.

I feel myself drifting away from you.

You will grow new wings, Momma.

That minivan with the mismatched doors will help you fly for now.

You have chocolate eyes and freckles just like me. And I am grateful to have dreamed with you even for just a little while. I just wish I could wake up and live those dreams with you now. We were constellations of misery pressed into a dark and desolate canvas. I had forgotten that the stars were still beautiful. I had forgotten that so were we.

Hope can't be a hollow wish or dream. It needs to be filled, levied, brimming over with intention and action and belief and reaching, reaching, reaching, stretching until your muscles ache because you want it that damn much, and you won't stop reaching until you hold it.

Until it is yours.

I let go too soon.

60

Life,

You were broken, often ugly, and always too much, but you also hid promises in pockets, tucked hope under mattresses, and crammed a thousand perfect moments between the shards of sharp and treacherous ones.

I am sorry I had forgotten them.

I am sorry I didn't even see.

And a breath too late, I realized . . .

I loved you.

Help Is Here.

These resources are meant to support you and help keep you safe. All are available 24-7/365. Don't keep your suffering secret. Seeking help is crucial to healing. Reach out if you or someone you know is hurting. There are many who have struggled and suffered with these issues. You are not alone. **If you are in immediate danger,** call 9-1-1.

For suicide prevention:
> *National Suicide Prevention Lifeline*
> *1-800-273-8255*
> suicidepreventionlifeline.org

> *Substance Abuse and Mental Health Services Administration*
> *National Hotline*
> *1-800-662-HELP (4357)*
> samhsa.gov

> *The notOK App*
> notokapp.com

For child abuse:

Childhelp National Child Abuse Hotline
1-800-422-4453
childhelp.org

For domestic violence:

National Domestic Violence Hotline
1-800-799-7233
thehotline.org

For free crisis support:

Crisis Text Line
Text HOME to 741741
crisistextline.org

Acknowledgments

This book was as devastating to write as it was healing. I wrote the very first raw, messy, and incoherent draft over the course of eleven days. Alone in the dark. I didn't want my husband to hear me sobbing over my computer. I didn't want to admit aloud what I was writing on each page: that I was hurting too. And that this story that bled out of me was in so many ways mine.

This book wouldn't have existed without Katie Selby's comment on the first page, written as a flash fiction piece online on World Suicide Prevention Day, insisting that it should be my book. I remember the feeling of fear, of dread, of *absolutely not!* And then I knew that this book had to be written because my heart ached at the mere thought of it. This book wouldn't have survived that first terrible draft without Becky Johnson. She was the first to read it and critique it and help me shape it into a story. She was the one who wrote notes in the margins that made me believe that this story mattered. There were so many others who saw this novel in its infancy and who anchored me in believing that Ellie's story was important. I kept going on this journey because of each and every one of them.

Holly McGhee, patron saint of author dreams and also my beloved agent, has been an absolute powerhouse of editorial insight. Her patience, love, care, and brilliance are a wonder. She gave this novel new life and was its fiercest advocate. I feel blessed to be a part of the extraordinary Pippin family.

On my very first call with Brian Geffen, I knew I wanted him as my editor. His enthusiasm and vision were so aligned with my own that I couldn't imagine a more perfect home for Ellie's story. His comments in the manuscript were my happy rocket fuel and made me feel so seen in my every intention for this novel. Between his and Rachel Murray's insights and edits, I felt we were able to wrestle with this difficult subject matter with sensitivity and heart. Brian has been steadfast in his devotion to this book, and I couldn't be more grateful.

And so much gratitude to the entire Holt/Macmillan Children's team! From the very first in-person meeting with Brian and Christian Trimmer, I felt home. I was paired with the amazing (and possibly long-lost awesome cousin) book designer Katie Klimowicz and the awesome artist Peony Yip. I was mind-boggled by my copy editor, Brenna Franzitta, and her exceptional attention to detail (I am quite certain that copy editors are unicorns) and my production editors, Melinda Ackell and Taylor Pitts. I also must sing praises to my phenomenal core publicity and marketing team: Kelsey Marrujo, Melissa Zar, Katie Quinn, Kristen Luby, and Gaby Salpeter! They crafted a plan so fully aligned with this book's mission, and I am in awe of their talent and effort. I also want to acknowledge all the people who sat around the table in the Macmillan office on that December day (and all those who have impacted this book's journey) for championing this story. I walked into that room and kept all of my tears of gratitude tucked away, but they were there. They still are.

I did revisions with my agent, got my book deal, and went through the editorial process on this novel while enrolled at the Vermont College of Fine Arts. While I didn't work on this novel while attending, I was able to transfer the skills I acquired to this manuscript. More importantly, I found my people. My fellow Guardians, I am so grateful that the stars led me to you all. You are some of the most exquisite and beautiful and generous humans I have ever met. You are magic.

Gina Loveless, my bookish bestie. Thank you for your squeals of pure joy whenever I tell you news, your ocean-deep compassion and understanding, and your never-ending badassery. They inspire me and I know I would've teetered into self-doubt more often without you. We are in this for the long haul and I feel so lucky to have you as my roller-coaster buddy.

Regina (thank you for letting me borrow your name!) and Shona, my soul squad. You both are creative goddesses.

You've been with me from the beginning and have been witness to some of my most life-changing moments and epiphanies. In fact, you often were vital in the manifestation of them. It is such a privilege to be your witness. It is an honor that you were mine. Thank you. For pushing me, loving me, celebrating me, and believing in me. Our moments together sparkle with magic.

Mama and Papa, your creative hearts left us a legacy of artistic love. I miss you so much, but when I need you, I feel you near. When I signed my contract, I surrounded myself with your handwriting and heirlooms because I knew none of this would have been possible without you.

Dad, you've become one of my most cherished cheerleaders and greatest friends. Your strength and support have meant so much to me. You've been such a source of comfort over these years. You are an amazing father and grandfather, and I am so happy that we have you in our lives. The #1 Papa Jorge and Daddio. Thank you for reminding me to focus on the important and to not be afraid to honor myself along the way. Lori, thank you for being such a beautiful addition to our family unit. You have braved so much and are such a testament of love. We are so lucky to have you in our lives.

Martina, my sister and chivi. You are so gloriously YOU and I am always taken aback by your heart, talent, and brilliance. Damn, woman. The world better get ready for you. I feel like I could make being proud of you my profession.

You never let me forget who I am and where my heart is leading me. Keep shining bright, love. The world needs you full blast. So do I.

Oh, my mama bear (aka the sasha). Where would I be without you? Not here at all. Your strength, audacious optimism, and beautiful openness to life are a marvel. You sacrificed, you loved, you gave and gave. For me. For us. For the dreams we wanted to make real. Our coffee table was the altar to all our hopes. I am blessed to be your daughter. We found our art and hearts at the same time. Thank you. You always told me to be unafraid of flying even when we felt lost in the dark. Look at our lives now. Storms have come, but we still have this wide-open blue sky. Let's fly higher. And as you soar, remember that your wings (and song) are beautiful.

Jese, mi vida, you make me laugh, you hold me up, you squeeze me tight. You have been the rock on which I have sharpened my blade and the foundation on which I can stand, sure and certain. You are my anchor when I feel unsteady and drifting, and your shoulder has been my refuge. You remind me that I am limitless and that nothing is impossible. You have given me our beautiful children and this life so full of love and devotion. You are strength, heart, love, power. I am humbled by your faith, hard work and sacrifice, and bright and tenacious spirit. You bring color to my life every day. I am proud of the man you have become and honored to have you by my side.

Gio, my little dragon. You kept your momma strong while I was on this journey. You showed me what I was capable of. You also taught me that sleep and cuddles should never be taken for granted and that it is very possible to live your happiest days hanging on smiles and baby giggles. Daddy and I waited a long time for you. Thank you for choosing us to be yours.

Juliette, my daughter, it is my greatest honor to be your mother. You are all heart and love and art. I remember how my whole life stuttered awake at the sound of your heartbeat. I started writing again because of you. I knew if I was going to ask you to live your dreams then it was time I started to live mine. Dream, my little wonder woman. And then live a life full of them. I love you.